William Berry Lapham

In Memoriam. Hon. Joseph R. Bodwell

governor of Maine

William Berry Lapham

In Memoriam. Hon. Joseph R. Bodwell
governor of Maine

ISBN/EAN: 9783337734091

Printed in Europe, USA, Canada, Australia, Japan

Cover: Foto ©Raphael Reischuk / pixelio.de

More available books at **www.hansebooks.com**

IN MEMORIAM.

Hon. Joseph R. Bodwell,

GOVERNOR OF MAINE.

Born June 18, 1818. Died December 15, 1887.

PUBLISHED BY ORDER OF THE GOVERNOR ᴬᴺᴰ COUNCIL.

AUGUSTA:
BURLEIGH & FLYNT, PRINTERS TO THE STATE.
1888.

STATE OF MAINE.

In Council. December 20, 1887.

Ordered, That a special committee be appointed to employ a suitable person to prepare a report of the ceremonies of the funeral of the late Governor Bodwell and have the same printed. Read and passed by the Council, and by the Governor approved.

ORAMANDAL SMITH,
Secretary of State.

STATE OF MAINE.

Council Chamber,
Augusta, December 29, 1887.

Dr. WM. B. LAPHAM, Augusta, Maine.

Dear Sir: The undersigned, a committee of the Council appointed by Governor Marble pursuant to the foregoing order, knowing your friendship for our late esteemed Governor Bodwell, and having confidence in your qualifications for such a duty, invite you to prepare a brief biographical sketch of our late Governor, an account of his sickness, death and funeral, with such tributes from the press, and resolutions of respect passed on the occasion, and such other matter as may be deemed appropriate, in manner and form to be printed.

Very Respectfully,

ELLIOTT WOOD,
GEO. M. WARREN, } *Committee.*
EBEN E. RAND,

BIOGRAPHICAL SKETCH.

Joseph Robinson Bodwell was born in Methuen, Mass., June 18, 1818, and was the tenth in a family of eleven children. The house where he and his brothers and sisters were born, situated in that part of Methuen which, in 1847, was set off and incorporated as Lawrence, is still standing in a good state of preservation. It is now owned by Mr. Fred Clark, agent of the Pemberton Mills, who has a residence opposite, and has been occupied for a number of years by teachers of the High School. This house, which was occupied by five generations of Bodwells, is an old-fashioned mansion house, similar to those erected quite generally by well-to-do New England farmers a hundred years ago. It is of good size, two stories high, and surrounded by grand old trees. One of these trees is said to have been set out the day before Governor Bodwell's father was born. Joseph Bodwell, father of the Governor, was a kind-hearted, generous man, was always cheerful, and had a pleasant word for every one who came beneath his roof-tree. Many a weary traveller found welcome and hospitality at his fireside and table. He was a man of influence, was one of the directors of the old Andover bridge across the Merrimack, possessed a sound judgment and his opinion was sought after and valued on many occasions. But he became involved in suits at law, lost money by signing notes for friends, and finally, in 1829, he sold the old place and removed to a less pretentious one in West Haverhill. He always predicted that there would be a city at the Falls, and lived to see it commenced. Mary How, the mother of Governor Bodwell, born January 17,

1771, daughter of Joseph and Hannah (Carlton) How, was a superior and cultured woman. Her family was always prominent and influential in Methuen, and her relatives supplied deacons for the Congregational church there for more than a century. She was a sister of the late Daniel How, a successful Portland merchant. Joseph Bodwell was a teamster as well as farmer, and engaged more or less in conveying wood, lumber and country produce to Salem, and later, to Lowell, bringing back merchandise for the traders in Methuen, Haverhill and Andover. He could turn his hand to almost anything, and this peculiarity was inherited by the late Governor.

Joseph R. Bodwell lived with his parents upon the Bodwell farm until he was eight years of age. His oldest sister, Mary, was now married to Patrick Flemming, who owned and occupied a farm in the western part of Methuen, about five miles from the Bodwell homestead. Joseph was her favorite brother, and when she became settled in her new home, she wished him to live with her, and he could easily be spared, for without him the family was still large. He lived with his sister eight years, at which time Patrick Flemming died. He had now developed into a sturdy youth, and already begun to exhibit many of those qualities which distinguished his maturer years. He thus early aspired to the ownership of real estate, and after the death of his brother-in-law, he and his father purchased of his sister and others, the Flemming farm. which was one of the best in that portion of the State. As his parents advanced in years, both being feeble and past labor, an arrangement was made, in 1848, by which they went to live with their daughter, Mrs. Asa Simonds, when the Flemming farm became the property of Joseph R. Bodwell and his brother Henry. The parents died before the close of the year 1848, with an interval of only three weeks between the dates of their deaths.

It was soon after the Bodwells purchased the Flemming farm that the attention of the Lawrences, and other Boston manufacturers and capitalists, was directed to the advantages of the falls upon the Merrimack river, within the town of Methuen, known as Bodwell's Falls, for manufacturing purposes. The land about the falls was soon purchased, building operations were at once commenced on an extensive scale, and the frame for the first house built under the new regime was furnished by Joseph R. and Henry Bodwell, who now owned and were operating a saw-mill in connection with their other business. The brothers were plowing in the field when Mr. Job Jenness came and desired them to furnish the frame for a house. With characteristic energy they repaired to the mill, sawed the timber for the frame, and the following day took it to Lawrence, a distance of five miles. When the dam across the Merrimack was being built, Joseph R. and Henry Bodwell were employed in hauling the granite from the quarries in Pelham, N. H., for its construction. It required an immense amount of stone for this purpose, and it was while thus employed that Governor Bodwell took his initial lesson in that business which became his life pursuit, and in which he achieved great success. He here became familiar with all the numerous processes involved in quarrying, handling and working granite, and it was at this period, while cultivating the Flemming farm, that he formed that attachment to agricultural pursuits and stock-raising which he never lost, and which became his pastime in later years. In process of time the brothers made a division of their property, Joseph R. taking the farm for his share, and Henry the mills. By greater care in its cultivation, the farm had become more productive and had greatly increased in value. In 1848, Mr. Bodwell was married and brought his wife to this farm, and here his family continued to reside until he moved to Hallowell, in 1866.

It was not poverty, as has frequently been stated, that caused Joseph R. Bodwell to leave the paternal roof at the tender age of eight years. His father had a large family, it is true, and his means had been somewhat reduced by the dishonesty of those whom he had befriended, but he was able to meet the demands of his household, and if they lacked some of the luxuries, as did most families in those days, his family certainly never wanted for any of the necessaries of life. He left home because his childless sister wanted him and needed his companionship, and he there received the full measure of a sister's affection. He assisted his brother-in-law upon the farm, aided his sister in her household duties, attended the district school, learned the cordwainer's trade, and devoted his evenings and mornings to mending and making shoes. This was a busy life for a boy, but it was characteristic of Joseph R. Bodwell, both as boy and man. He was early noted for honesty, perseverance, economy and thrift, and these sterling qualities became leading traits in his character. He developed physical as well as mental strength, and thus, with mind and body evenly balanced, in his maturer manhood he possessed great powers of endurance, and was able to execute the business projects which his fertile and active mind conceived and matured. As has been appropriately said of another distinguished New Englander who came up from the lower walks of life and attained to the highest honors, " the defects of his scholarship, the laborious period of his youth, and the humble avocations of his early manhood, were favorable to his fortunes." In the case of Governor Bodwell, they seemed to keep him on a level with the masses of the people, and enabled him to understand and interpret their desires and purposes with accuracy. He early developed in a marked degree that peculiar assemblage of physical, mental and moral qualities so requisite to the successful management of great business enterprises, requiring the employment of large numbers of men.

In 1852 in company with Hon. Moses Webster, who deceased at Rockland about a year ago, Governor Bodwell came to Maine. They had been friends in Massachusetts, had worked together at the Pelham quarries, both in their earlier years had worked at shoemaking, and besides they were remotely related, though it is doubtful if either of them was ever aware of this fact. It was in this way. Henry Bodwell, the ancestor of the Governor, married Bethiah, daughter of John

Emery, Jr., of Newbury, whose mother was Mary, daughter of John Webster of Ipswich, and John Webster was therefore the common ancestor of Moses Webster and Joseph R. Bodwell, about six generations back. Under the firm name of Bodwell and Webster, they commenced operating in granite, in a small way, having their headquarters upon the South Fox Island, now the sea-girt town of Vinalhaven in Penobscot Bay. At their small beginning, it is said that Mr. Bodwell drove the ox team used in moving the granite, and shod the animals with his own hands. From this small starting point, sprang wondrous results. Soon the business increased, the firm name became Bodwell, Webster and Company, and capital sought investment in the new enterprize.

The next change was the organization of the Bodwell Granite Company with a sufficient capital, and leading business men to aid in the management of its affairs, but the moving and master spirit from the very first was Joseph R. Bodwell, who, soon after he came to Maine, was recognized as the leading granite man of the United States. He was chosen the first president of the Company and held that position to the day of his death. Under his prudent and energetic management, it became the leading granite corporation in the country. Mr. Bodwell had long felt the need, in his business operations, of granite of a lighter color and finer texture than that which he had quarried at Vinalhaven, for monumental work, and for artistic designs in architecture. The Hallowell granite presented all these rare qualities, and in 1866, Mr. Bodwell moved his family from Methuen to Hallowell, and a little later, organized the Hallowell Granite Company, of which he was made president and chief executive officer. Soon after the Company was organized the business assumed huge proportions. The products of the association have been sent into almost every State in the Union. Its colossal statuary, rivalling in durability and beauty the finest marble, is to be found in all our great cities from Portland to New Orleans, and it has an increasing and widely extending demand. The following list embraces some of the more prominent buildings and monuments which have been constructed from the product of the quarries of the two associations of which Mr. Bodwell was president :

New State, War and Navy Departments Building, Washington, D. C. ; Masonic Temple, Record building, and Pennsylvania R. R. Passenger Station, &c., Philadelphia ; new Court House and Post Office, Atlanta, Ga. ; new Custom House and Post Office, Cincinnati, Ohio ; new County and City Building, new Board of Trade Building, Offices for Pullman Co., Counselman Building, Home Insurance Co. Building, Chicago, Ill. ; St. Louis Bridge, Missouri ; New York and Brooklyn Bridge, Welles Building, Mutual Life Insurance Company Building, Manhattan Bank Building, Kelley Building, &c., New York ; Wellington Building, Jordan, Marsh & Co. Building, &c., Boston ; new Custom House and Post Office, Fall River, Mass. ; Peabody Town Buildings, Peabody, Mass., &c. ; Gen. Wool Monument, Troy, N. Y. ; Pilgrim Monument, Plymouth, Mass. ; Yorktown Monument ; Smith Monument, Philadelphia, Pa. ; mausoleum and monument for Dr. Gibson, Jamestown, Pa., &c. ; new Post Office and Custom House, Brooklyn, N. Y. ; basement of new Post Office and Court House at Erie, Penn. ; North Western Insurance Co. Building, Milwaukee, Wis. ; polished granite for the State House, Indianapolis, Indiana, ; New York Equitable Life Building, New York City ; State Capitol Building, Albany, N. Y. ; West Museum of Art Building, New York City ; mausoleum for Governor Fenton of Jamestown, New York, &c., &c. The Sphynx in Mount Auburn Cemetery, a stupendous monument, was quarried and cut at Hallowell. This list embraces only some of the larger operations undertaken and completed by the two companies. The minor contracts for soldiers' monuments and other monumental work are far too many to be enumerated here. But the list given is sufficient to indicate the vast amount of responsibility which rested upon Governor Bodwell as the chief business manager, and the successful completion of all these numerous contracts, involving the outlay of many millions, shows business tact and ability of a very high order. It involved the constant employment of a small army of workmen, including first class artists and artisans, and workers of every grade. The two corporations under Governor Bodwell's management never found any difficulty in the employment of help. They never had any strikers among their workmen, and a good man once in their employ never thought of leaving it. From his own experience, Governor Bodwell knew how to sympathize with the laboring classes. He interested himself in their individual prosperity, and men in his employ soon came to regard him as their personal friend.

The active mind of Governor Bodwell, not content with the business intrusted to him by the two great granite companies, sought investment and profit in other enterprises. He had interests in ice and lumbering on the Kennebec, in land, lumbering and milling operations on the Penobscot, in several water supply companies, and in a projected line of railway between New York and Boston. A minor operation but one which promised important results, was the development of a sea-side resort at Cape Small Point on the coast of Maine. He never lost his interest in agriculture, and soon after he came to Hallowell, he purchased a fine farm in the suburbs of that city, which he improved and enlarged from time to time, by purchase, until he possessed one of the best and most productive farms on the Kennebec. A few years ago, he purchased for a small sum an old and run-down farm situated some five miles west of Hallowell, of one of his workmen who had failed to get a living from it. It contained a large area of bog-land, the bed of an ancient pond, and by draining and other improvements, under Governor Bodwell's direction, it soon became one of the best stock farms in the county.

In 1879, in partnership with Mr. Hall C. Burleigh, Governor Bodwell commenced the importation of pure-bred stock, and this was continued for several years. The importations embraced Hereford, Polled Angus and Sussex cattle, and Shropshire and Dorset sheep. This was not entered into as a money-making enterprise on the part of Governor Bodwell, but as a pastime from more arduous duties, and as a means of assisting a friend. The business was eminently successful, and not only served its original purpose of an amusement or diversion, but it was a source of financial gain, of great importance, at least to one of the partners, and also accomplished a great amount of good in the improvement of stock in many parts of the country. They sold animals from their farms in Hallowell and Vassalborough all over New England, into several of the Middle States, and no small part of their importations went to improve the breeds on the great stock ranches and ranges of the far west.

Governor Bodwell was not a politician in the ordinary meaning of the term, but he always took a deep interest in public affairs, and few men had a clearer appreciation of what constitutes true American citizenship. He never sought official distinction, but office was sometimes thrust upon him. Twice he served in the lower branch of the Maine Legislature as representative from the city of Hallowell, where his vigorous manhood and excellent financial judgment, as well as other sterling qualities, were quickly recognized, and gave him a high standing in this popular branch of the State Government. For two terms also, by virtue of the almost unanimous suffrage of her citizens, he served as mayor of his adopted city of Hallowell. His name was mentioned in connection with the gubernatorial office some years before he would consent to become a candidate. A few years ago he told the writer that he had been approached upon the subject by leading and influential men of his party, but he said most emphatically that he did not want the office, that his time was so taken up with his large business interests that he could not afford to be Governor. But being constantly importuned, in 1886, reluctantly, as many well know, he consented to have his name presented to the nominating convention. It only required this to insure a unanimous nomination, and an election by a very large majority. After his inauguration, the public well know with what modesty he assumed the great trusts imposed upon him, and with what fidelity he administered the affairs of the government. Simple in his habits, easily approachable, a patient listener, prompt to decide and act, courteous even in his refusals, he won the esteem and respect of all with whom he came in official contact. The eulogiums gathered from the press of the State, and reprinted in another place, indicate the esteem and regard in which he was held by all, without regard to party. He was decided in his convictions of official duty, and all his acts as Governor strongly bear his impress.

In private life Governor Bodwell's character was above reproach. During the exciting gubernatorial campaign, when, if a candidate has any defects, or has been guilty of any lapses, they are sure to be brought against him, and when it is frequently the case that false accusations are made for partisan purposes, no word was written or spoken affecting the good name of Governor Bodwell, and he was opposed on party grounds alone. Honest in his dealings with mankind, acquiring wealth only by legitimate means, he was generous in his impulses and his private benefactions were many. He also contributed liberally of his means in aid of public charities, in support of educational institutions and for the cause of religion. In his quiet, unostentatious way, he was constantly aiding those whom sickness or adverse fortune had made needy, and the poor of Hallowell were among his most devoted friends. His nature was sympathetic, and in his intercourse with those with whom business or office brought him in contact, he was invariably courteous and kind. The members of his council and his military staff recognized him not only as their official head, but his demeanor toward them was such that they soon regarded him as a personal friend, and interested in everything pertaining to their welfare. This is why these officials and all associated with him in the State Government, as well as hosts of friends, regard the death of Governor Bodwell as a personal bereavement.

In religious belief Governor Bodwell was a Universalist, but he was free from bigotry, and was a Christian in the broadest sense of the word. He had faith in our religious institutions, and believed in giving them a cheerful and liberal support. He was a member of the Board of Trustees of Westbrook Seminary, and often contributed liberally to its funds. He believed in temperance and in the enforcement of the laws against the infamous traffic in intoxicating drinks. No previous Governor of Maine had manifested so much interest in this matter, and while he thereby made enemies of parties in interest, the law-abiding citizens of the State, and all those whose support is of any value, were rallying around him. He believed in kindness to dumb animals, and nothing vexed him more than their abuse, either from lack of food, from overloading, or from the unreasonable application of the whip or goad, by those in his employ. He made it a practice to caution all newly hired teamsters that their term of office would depend very much upon the treatment of the animals committed to their care. His kind and sympathetic nature rebelled against the ill-treatment of either animal or person. He was especially kind to the young, and among his sincerest mourners are little children, to whom he has spoken words of encouragement or aided in a more material way. He received his friends with generous, old-fashioned hospitality, and with no useless forms and ceremonies. In his family he was kind and indulgent, gratifying every reasonable desire, a model husband and father. The loss of a man possessing these grand qualities, even from the quiet walks of life, is keenly felt, but when a public man, one so intimately connected with our material interests of business and government, is suddenly removed by death, it creates a void not easily filled, and causes a whole State to mourn.

Governor Bodwell enjoyed robust health, rarely losing a day from sickness. He had naturally a strong constitution, and his early physical training, and life in the open air, combined with strictly temperate habits, kept his physical system in excellent condition. His fatal sickness, therefore, coming upon him so suddenly, without premonition, striking him down in the vigor and strength of well matured manhood, was to many almost unaccountable. On the 5th day of December Governor and Mrs. Bodwell took the cars at Hallowell, intending to go to Rockland, and while away his purpose was to make an official visit to the State Prison at Thomaston. Arriving at Brunswick, and while waiting for the Bath train, having taken Mrs. Bodwell to the ladies' room, the Governor went out to meet some gentlemen who had expressed a desire to converse with him on some matters of business. He had been out only a few moments, when a waiter from the dining room came in, and, motioning for Mrs. Bodwell to come out, he informed her that the Governor had been taken suddenly ill. When she reached the dining room she found him sitting by a table and leaning over it, his face deadly pale, with great beads of perspiration covering his forehead, and suffering the keenest anguish through the chest, left shoulder and left arm. A messenger was instantly despatched for Dr. Alfred Mitchell of the Maine Medical School, and he was soon in attendance upon the Governor. He pronounced it *angina pectoris*,* a very dangerous disease, and one of the most painful known to the medical profession. By the application of the proper remedies, the Governor soon had temporary relief.

Governor Bodwell had every needed attention while at Brunswick, and remained there until the arrival of the afternoon train, when a bed was extemporized on board, and he was brought to his home in Hallowell. It fortunately happened that his family physician, Dr. W. L. Thompson, (homeopathic) was on this train, and, having assisted his patient home, he afterward, with the assistance of his son, Dr. W. S. Thompson, took charge of the case. Dr. Mitchell of Brunswick called once, and Dr. George E. Brickett of Augusta, twice during his sickness, at the request of the family, but the case continued in charge of the Doctors Thomp-

---

* Literally, "anguish in the breast." This is the disease of which Charles Sumner died. The precise nature of the disease is not very well known. It is generally connected with some morbid condition of the heart, and is called sometimes neuralgia of the heart. The first attack is sometimes fatal, and it is the opinion of Dr. Thompson that but for the prompt and vigorous treatment of Dr. Mitchell, Governor Bodwell would have died at Brunswick.

son until the end. Under their treatment he improved, and Tuesday night was free from pain. He remained better until Thursday noon following, when he had another severe attack of pain in the region of the heart. This was relieved by his physician, and after that time he suffered scarcely any pain. His tongue cleared, his appetite was soon restored, and his family and friends felt confident of a speedy recovery. From Friday, the 9th, to Monday, the 12th, he continued to improve, and rested well at night. Then he began to have restless nights, would lose his breath on dropping off to sleep, and required a frequent change of position. He continued much the same through Tuesday night and Wednesday. On Wednesday evening he felt encouraged, and dictated a telegram to a friend stating that he "felt himself on the upgrade." During the early part of the night he was somewhat restless, but had occasional short intervals of sleep. At three o'clock he was helped to his easy chair, reclining in which, he had two hours of quiet, refreshing sleep. At five he awoke and asked to be conducted to his bed. He remained there only a few minutes, when he wished to be returned to his chair and exclaimed, "Get me there quickly." These were his last words. His attendants aided him in reaching his chair, but before being seated he dropped back into it and expired without a groan or a struggle—a painless death. He died at 5.30 A. M., Dec. 15th. The particulars of his sickness were kindly furnished by Dr. Thompson, who pronounces the immediate cause of his death to have been "heart failure," and the more remote cause, congestion of the anterior left lung from a cold contracted on the night of Friday, December 2d, while the Governor was returning from Boston.

It is the opinion of the writer that Governor Bodwell overtasked himself, and that overwork had much to do with bringing on the fatal disease. There will be those who think differently, but some of his most intimate friends coincide with this view. All will agree that there is a limit to human endurance, and Governor Bodwell certainly had business cares and responsibilities sufficient for any one man before he became Governor. His time for years had all been occupied, and he gave himself scarcely any vacations or periods of rest. He was obliged to spend more or less of his time in traveling upon business matters, and was necessarily somewhat irregular in taking his meals and in his hours of sleep. It was a marvel to those acquainted with his immense business responsibilities, and the enforced irregularities in his mode of living required in its prosecution, how he could bear up under the constant tension, and continue so apparently robust and healthy. His naturally strong constitution, his powerful muscular development, his life-long total abstinence from the inebriating cup, and his indomitable will, all conspired to keep up his health and strength. But Governor Bodwell had arrived at that age when the powers of life, under the most favorable circumstances, begin to weaken, and when, instead of assuming more and greater responsibilities, it is the duty of every business man to begin to relieve himself of those which he already has. Governor Bodwell had thought of this and talked of it, but he had not yet found the place where he thought he could begin to curtail his business or transfer his responsibilities to other hands.

He allowed himself to be elected Governor of Maine, and no man ever assumed the duties of the gubernatorial office with a higher sense of its responsibilities. A residence in the State of nearly forty years had made him familiar with her great material interests, and the day he was elected he began to take measures to render himself familiar with the State institutions, with a view to intelligent administration of State affairs. He gave largely of his time to these objects, and still kept pace with the demands of his private business. When he was inaugurated, he was all ready to assume the duties of his office, and Maine never had a more conscientious, painstaking chief magistrate. The duties of Governor are more arduous than formerly, and the calls upon his time increase from year to year. No great public occasion is now considered complete without his presence and co-operation.

2

These duties, with the demands of his ever increasing business, kept Governor Bodwell almost constantly on the move. Then there have been petty annoyances which are inseparable from the gubernatorial office, misrepresentation of his acts and perversion of his motives, which are always more or less annoying. As chief executive of the State, he felt it his duty to see that the laws were enforced against crime. The prohibitory law, which had not only been upon the statute books from the time when he first came to Maine, but had recently been made a part of the organic law of the State, and which, by non-enforcement, was becoming a by-word and a reproach, he determined to have enforced, and he went about it with characteristic energy, and every prospect of success. But the manifold duties of the gubernatorial office added only so much more to his previous cares, and while he claimed to bear up under his accumulated responsibilities, with health unimpaired, his friends, or most of them, felt that the strain was too much. He had not looked as well as formerly, and his face sometimes bore a care-worn appearance which made his friends anxious. In September, just before starting for Philadelphia to attend the Centennial Celebration of the Constitution, he had an attack of severe pain in his left shoulder and arm, which may probably be regarded as the precursor of the more serious attack at Brunswick, two months later. While his active mind was wholly engaged in the performance of his manifold duties, a fatal disease had been insidiously developing and hastened by the exposure and severe cold, as well as other complications mentioned by Dr. Thompson, it speedily carried him off. The case of Governor Bodwell presents an illustration and a warning. It illustrates the too close application and intense energy of our leading business men, and it is a warning that those God-given powers of mind and body with which they are blessed cannot be over-taxed with impunity, more especially by those who are far along on the down grade of life.

There is not much space for eulogy here, nor is eulogy necessary in this case. The respect in which Governor Bodwell was held while living, and the universal regret manifested at his death, are more potent and convincing than mere words. He performed well his part in life. He entered upon no official position without first acquainting himself with its duties, and then he unhesitatingly took upon himself the responsibilities of administration. He asked advice of those in whom he had confidence, but when he came to act, it was in accordance with his own convictions of right and duty. He was a born leader, and there could be no greater mistake than to suppose that he was, or could be, led by others. He was not trained to public speaking, nor schooled in debate, but when his duty as Governor required him to respond to a sentiment, or to speak at the anniversaries of public institutions, or at other public gatherings to which he had been invited, he did it with a facility that surprised his friends, and even himself. His words were always well chosen, fitly spoken, and his remarks, though brief, were always to the point. In his intercourse with Governors and officials of other states, as he was called upon to have upon several occasions during his brief term of office, his bearing was dignified and consistent with the high position he held and the sovereign State he represented. And now as he passes into the domain of history, with his life work done, and nobly done, he will be recorded as one of Maine's foremost and most valued citizens, and as one of her most conscientious chief magistrates.

HOW THE SAD NEWS WAS RECEIVED.

The news of Governor Bodwell's sudden demise was soon wired over the State and produced a profound sensation. From reports sent out the day previous, it was confidently believed he would recover. His death occurred too late in the morning to appear in the morning papers, and from the telegraphic offices of the cities and large towns, the sad intelligence passed from one to another, and the deepest grief was depicted upon every face. Reporters rushed to Hallowell, and during the remainder of the day, every available scrap of intelligence bearing upon the case was gathered up and sent to the various daily papers in, and to many out of the State. The family of the illustrious dead was overwhelmed with their great affliction, and the whole city wore a pall of sorrow and sadness. "He was our greatest and best friend," was repeated on every hand. The gloom settled heavily over the school children, and their sad faces, as they walked silently along the streets and glanced toward the office of the Hallowell Granite Company and toward the desolate house, showed evidence of heartfelt sorrow. In Augusta, the Court adjourned, and as the news spread, all the courts of justice in the State, then in session, took the same action. Telegrams of sorrow for the dead and sympathy for the family came pouring in from all parts of the country, from friends of the deceased, and from State governments.

At the State House, the intelligence caused the keenest regrets. Grief choked the utterance of many, and every face was expressive of the deepest sorrow. It became the duty of the Secretary of State to notify Hon. Sebastian S. Marble, President of the Senate, who, by the provisions of the Constitution, became acting or *ex-officio* Governor from the moment of the death of Governor Bodwell. Mr. Marble arrived in Augusta on the evening train of that day. The members of the Executive Council were summoned to Augusta, and with sad hearts assembled at the Council Chamber on the day succeeding Governor Bodwell's death. The relations between Governor and Council had been uncommonly confidential and pleasant, and when he was stricken down by disease, the members of the Council felt much more than an official interest in his recovery. From reports received from the sickroom, they had every reason to believe that he was convalescing and would soon be able to rejoin them, and the report of the fatal termination of his disease was received by all with great surprise and filled them with transports of grief. Acting Governor Marble officially notified the people of the State of the death of Governor Bodwell by issuing the following circular :

STATE OF MAINE.

EXECUTIVE DEPARTMENT,
AUGUSTA, December 16, 1887.

It is with deep sorrow and regret that I announce to the people of the State the death of Governor Joseph R. Bodwell, which occurred at his residence in Hallowell, Dec. 15th, at 5 30 o'clock A. M.

In his many years of active business life, his wide circle of personal friends, and his yet wider circle of business acquaintances have learned to love and respect him for his manly, generous character, and in his brief official career he has endeared himself to all the citizens of this State.

The body will lie in state at the capitol from Sunday noon until the funeral, which will take place at the State House on Tuesday, Dec. 20th, at 11 A. M. I have already designated committees of the Senate and House of Representatives to participate in the exercises. I now invite all who may desire to do so to be present at the funeral services. I desire that all public offices be closed on that day between the hours of 11 and 2 o'clock, and request that all business be suspended during that time so far as practicable, as a tribute of respect to our late chief magistrate.

SEBASTIAN S. MARBLE.

The Maine Militia were also notified in General Orders as follows :

HEADQUARTERS MAINE MILITIA,
ADJUTANT GENERAL'S OFFICE,
AUGUSTA, December 16, 1887.

GENERAL ORDERS,
No. 19.

The Governor and Commander-in-Chief announces with profound sorrow the death of his distinguished predecessor, JOSEPH R. BODWELL, which occurred at his home in Hallowell, Thursday morning, December 15th, instant, at 5 30. Governor Bodwell's life has been a bright and inspiring record of purity and fidelity in social and business relations, and integrity and ability in exacting and trying official position. He was a man whose impulses and inclinations were to kindliness, to truth and right. He was a faithful, generous and steadfast helper of friends, and an able and upright guardian of public good. Governor Bodwell's death is peculiarly saddening, in that it has come so suddenly. It has come at the end of a life of great accomplishments. It is a desolation to family and friends that no form of words can describe. It is a loss to the State that cannot be estimated But there is relief to the deep sorrow, to the heavy sense of loss. We can all believe that when death came to so good a man, the portals of the eternal world were arched with the radiant bow of promise.

II. In honor of the memory of the distinguished dead, and in special recognition of his earnest and helpful devotion to the interests of the militia, it is ordered that the colors of the several regiments and the guidon of the artillery be draped in mourning, and all officers will wear the usual badge of mourning upon the left arm and upon the sword hilt for the ensuing thirty days.

BY COMMAND OF SEBASTIAN S. MARBLE,
Governor and Commander-in-Chief.

S. J. GALLAGHER,
Adjutant General.

PREPARATION FOR THE LAST SAD RITES.

The State officials had a conference with the family, and it was decided to have a private funeral at the late home of the deceased in Hallowell, on Sunday, the 18th, after which the remains should be conveyed to the State House, there to lie in state until Tuesday, the 20th, when the public obsequies should be had. Meantime, a responsible duty rested upon General Harris, Superintendent of Public Buildings, that of putting the State House in order and having it properly draped. The draping was very elaborate, and was done under the direction of Capt. Geo. E. Brown of Portland. Black draperies covered the windows upon the portico, and the transom above the door, and as one entered the door, he felt that he was passing into the house of mourning. The fountain in the centre of the rotunda had been removed, and upon the site of it, between the four large central pillars, upon a raised platform covered with black draperies, was erected the catafalque. It was covered with black broadcloth and decorated with silver fringe and silver stars. From the large chandelier above, broad streamers of black crape and white thibet festooned to opposite sides of the room formed a canopy over the catafalque. The doors leading from the rotunda were draped in crape, with the exception of the main entrance, where two large flags were used, caught in at the sides with crape loops. The windows were curtained with flags. Festoons of black crape and white thibet hung about the sides of the room. On the right side of the rotunda, heavily draped in mourning was a large crayon portrait of Governor Bodwell. The large pillars of the rotunda were encased in crape, and festooned with smilax and silver stars. The corridors and stairways were draped in black. The Council Chamber was also filled with signs of mourning. The Governor's desk was draped in mourning and the edges fringed with smilax. Upon the table was the Governor's ebony gavel, decorated with white ribbons. In the Governor's private room, the same evidences of bereavement were seen. The table and chair were in mourning, and the room looked mournfully silent and sad. Representatives' Hall was also appropriately draped.

THE PRIVATE FUNERAL.

Governor Bodwell was a Free Mason, having joined Rockland Lodge, February 14, 1859, and the several lodges in the vicinity turned out in large numbers to escort the remains of their late brother from Hallowell to the State House, when the private funeral should be over. At ten o'clock Sunday morning, the citizens of Hallowell met at the City Hall and chose Col. D. P. Livermore as Marshal of the citizens' escort to Augusta. The Masonic Lodges of Hallowell, Gardiner and Augusta formed in line, after the arrival of the special trains, and marched to the Governor's late residence. Samuel B. Glazier officiated as Superintendent of the funeral, and the religious services were performed by Mr. Bodwell's pastor, Rev. J. S. Gledhill of Gardiner, who pronounced the following feeling and touching eulogy:

This whole life is walked under a shadow. Mystery hangs over everything. We do not understand anything about us. But the greatest mystery of it all is the dark fact of death. Into its shadow and darkness I come to you, dear friends, to say words of comfort and consolation. What I shall say will not take away your darkness, nor perhaps allay your grief. But I pray that the few words I speak may be to you as glints of light amidst the darkness, which shall help you to place your feet in the next step of your journey.

There have always been two ideas about death held by the minds of men. The earliest idea was that death was a covered way which led the soul into a silent region of shadows and darkness, where were gathered all those who passed out of the earthly life.

This view was later modified by the ideas of a division of this region of shadows into two parts, one of light and one of darkness, where were received into the one all the souls of the good in life, and into the other the souls of the evil. A further modification led to the idea of some mysterious change necessary to be made in the soul during life, or, in its absence, at death the soul was plunged into this hopeless darkness and despair.

But later came the more hopeful and rational view of death, which was that death is but the door which opens for the soul into another room of the Father's house of many mansions. And this is eminently the Christian view of death. Christ, the Redeemer, says: "In My Father's house are many mansions, if it were not so I would have told you. I go to prepare a place for you." And this view of death is further expressed by the apostle when he exclaims, "For we know that if our earthly house of this tabernacle were dissolved we have a building of God, a house not made with hands, eternal in the heavens."

There is stamped indelibly upon the heart and soul of every man an inherent sense that human destiny is ensphered in a divine order. This last view of death quickened this latent sense in men's hearts and taught them that the profound mystery out of which their life issues does not end in an abyss of nothingness. It taught men that death does not end all. Beyond death lies a future which to the rightly poised soul is not only without terror, but is full of beckoning peace. In that future as well as in the present the all-loving and all-blessing goodness of God encompasses the soul. This view of death also furnishes us with the ground and justification for that deep peace which in disappointment and loss stays itself on the assurance of ultimate triumph.

Now, I can only hint at the great thing of which I desire you to think, the great thing which I would that you keep in your hearts, faith that God always has a good and loving reason for what he does. And by this faith I do not mean an unreasoning acceptance of a dogma; nothing of the kind. Any faith that is real and living and true bases itself in and must grow out of the experiences of the world. And the experiences of the world have given us just such a God as this faith points to in whom to trust.

It is hardly necessary for me to point out to you that he whom you idolized as husband and father and brother, our beloved friend and neighbor, the estimable citizen and honored chief executive, drew the inspiration of his life from this same faith in God. Joseph R. Bodwell was an eminent Christian. He held an unwavering faith in the universal and unchanging love and goodness of God to all men. From this faith he drew the sweetness an l light and love which made him an idol in the home circle. From this same faith came that unusual degree of charity and patience which he felt and exercised for all who came in contact with him, or with whom he had in any way to deal. This same faith gave him that which so eminently distinguished him as a citizen and neighbor, an ever readiness to help and an open hearted generosity and sympathy with every form of need.

As a public official his courageous maintenance of what he deemed to be right and for the best interests of the people had its root in his great faith in the universal triumph of righteousness and truth, and gave him distinguished honor among the great men of our country.

As a source of comfort and consolation the thought of these things will yield you richness in the days of grief and darkness to come. In addition to this also, what treasures will not your memories hold of the beloved? That you were permitted to live in so intimate and tender relations with a nature so noble and so benignant must always be a cause for gratitude to the giver of all good things.

As a husband and father he was all that heart could wish, true, tender, affectionate and indulgent, shedding joy and gladness upon all the household.

It does not become me upon this occasion, even if time permitted, to speak at length of the eminent virtues of your beloved dead. I desire only to call to mind briefly these things and urge you to cherish the great faith which was the light and joy of his life, for your own comfort and consolation. Put your confidence in God who faileth not, and wait patiently for the deathless reunion which will surely be yours in the life to come. God leads us all out into the darkness, but only that we may go up into His clearer light.

> "There is no death, what seems so is transition.
> This life of mortal breath,
> Is but a suburb of the life elysian,
> Whose portals we call death"

At the close of the services the procession was formed, and moved to the State House in the following order :

Hacks, with relatives of the deceased.
Hearse with pall bearers, eight men, who were:
Hermon Lodge, Gardiner, No. 32: Daniel C. Palmer and Augustus Bailey.
Augusta Lodge No. 141: Charles C. Hunt and S. L. Boardman.
Bethlehem Lodge No. 35: E. C. Allen and Hon. George E. Weeks.
Hacks, with friends and relatives.
Hermon Lodge No. 32, F. & A. M., of Gardiner, 37 men.
Augusta Lodge No. 141, of Augusta.
Kennebec Lodge No. 5, of Hallowell.
Bethlehem Lodge No. 35, of Augusta.
Citizens in double file and in carriages.

At half past eleven the Capital Guards, in full dress, took up their quarters at the State House, as a guard of honor. On the arrival of the procession, the casket containing the remains was borne into the rotunda and placed upon the catafalque, the Masons escorting the body forming in line at the foot and side of the casket. Governor Marble, the Executive Council and the State officers were upon the opposite side, near the head of the casket. Then followed the impressive Masonic funeral service, at the close of which A. M. Spear, of Gardiner, advancing to the head of the casket, addressed Governor Marble in the following words :

Governor Marble:—We appear before you to-day as Masons, escorting to your care all that remains of a loved and respected brother, whose form now lies before us clothed in the habiliments of death.

His immediate relatives and friends, in grief and sorrow, have laid upon the altar of his memory their last sad tribute of love and affection. And now we stand here charged with the solemn duty imposed upon us by the mystic ties of the order, and the request of his friends, of consigning his body to the State for the reception of those public honors to which, both as an eminent citizen and its chief executive, he is so justly entitled.

As a man, he was of the highest character, spotless in integrity, unblemished in honor, boundless in generosity, using his wealth with lavish hand for the benefit of the community and the welfare of the State.

As a Mason, he exemplified in his daily life and conduct those noble virtues which the precepts of the order inculcate.

As an official, although called to the highest position in the gift of the people without any desire on his own part, for political preferment, he nevertheless assumed the duties of Governor with that same untiring energy and zeal which had in so marked a degree characterized his business career, devoting his very life to the progress and welfare of the State. His loss to the community, the fraternity and the State, is one which time cannot repair nor the lapse of years efface.

But his life work is done. And now in behalf of his relatives and friends and this fraternity, I deliver him through you to the care and custody of this commonwealth which he loved and which loved him so well.

To which Governor Marble made the following response:

In behalf of the State of Maine, I receive within its Capitol, the remains of its beloved and lamented late chief magistrate.

Within these walls, one short year ago, Joseph R. Bodwell was inaugurated Governor of Maine. To-day the portals of the Capitol are swung open to receive his lifeless form that here for a brief period it may lie in state before we consign it to its last resting place.

Living and dead, Maine honors this Nature's nobleman, whose character was as strong and heart as true as the granite hills he contended with and subdued. But in this hour of our great sorrow there is one thought of comfort; he died as the strong man always wishes to die, with the harness on, in the thickest of the fight, and in the full vigor of life. He is dead; but the example he leaves of what a poor boy, unaided, with only a strong arm and a brave heart, may accomplish, will live to cheer and encourage the youth of our State long after we of this generation shall have crossed the "isthmus between the two oceans."

He is at rest. Grandly has he fought the battle of life to the end, and we may devoutly believe that the words, "well done, good and faithful servant," will be spoken to him in

Heaven, even as they are spoken of him in thousands of homes on earth.

And may God grant to us who are living strength and wisdom to emulate the virtues of him whose body the State sorrowfully and tenderly now takes to its keeping.

LYING IN STATE.

The remains of Governor Bodwell were embalmed, and while lying in state, were viewed by large numbers of people from various parts of the State. The arrangements for the public funeral were placed in the hands of a committee, consisting of Councillor Seth M. Carter, Gen. George L. Beal and Col. George C. Wing. Capt. George D. Bisbee was selected as Chief Marshal. The following order was issued from the office of the Adjutant General :

HEADQUARTERS MAINE MILITIA, }
ADJUTANT GENERAL'S OFFICE,
AUGUSTA, December 17. 1887. }

GENERAL ORDERS, }
No. 20. }

I. Commanders of Companies A, B, C and E, of 1st Regiment, and D, E, G, and H. 2nd Regiment, M. V. M., and 1st and 2nd Platoons Battery, will report to Col. John J. Lynch, at Augusta, Tuesday A. M., Dec. 20th, with 32 Privates and Coporals. and File Closers. armed and equipped in full dress uniform with overcoats and white gloves.

II. A Special Military Train will leave as follows: Portland at 7.30 A. M., Lewiston, lower station, at 7.30, connecting at Brunswick with the special from Portland. Bangor at 7.30. Company E, 2nd Reg't, will take regular train, 8.20 A. M., and return on the regular P. M. train. Company H, 2nd Reg't, will leave on regular 9.15 train. All Companies but E, 2nd Reg't, will return home by special train Tuesday.

III. Colonel John J. Lynch, 1st Regiment, with Staff, will command the Military Escort.

The troops will be given dinner at Granite Hall, Augusta, at 11.30.

The National Home Band will furnish the music.

The senior officers on these trains will take command of the troops while en route to Augusta and return, and be held responsible for the behavior of the men.

IV. Commanding officer of Company F, 1st Regiment, will report at State House, Sunday, Dec. 18th, at 12 o'clock, with 25 men with officers in full dress uniform, armed and equipped for guard duty. This detail will also act as a guard of honor while the remains are being borne to the cemetery.

V. A gun will be fired at every half-hour, beginning at sunrise and ending at sunset.

Nineteen minute-guns will be fired while the remains are being borne to the place of interment.

After the remains are deposited in the grave, a salute of nineteen guns will be fired, in addition to three salvos of artillery.

BY ORDER OF THE COMMANDER-IN-CHIEF.

S. J. GALLAGHER,
Adjutant General.

Chief Marshal Bisbee issued the following circular:

OFFICE OF CHIEF MARSHAL,
AUGUSTA, Dec. 19, 1887.

Services in Representatives' Hall at 11 o'clock A. M.

1. Music — Prof. Thieme, Togus Military Band.
2. Reading of Scripture and Prayer, — Rev. A. F. Skeele, Augusta.
3. Selection, — Chickering Quartette, Augusta.
4. Address, — Rev. G. A. Hayden, Auburn.
5. Selection, — Chickering Quartette and Mrs. Milliken.
6. Benediction, — Rev. J. S. Gledhill, Gardiner.

The procession will form immediately after the services as follows:
Platoon of Police.
Chief Marshal and Aids.
Chief Marshal, George D. Bisbee, Buckfield.
Chief of Staff, H. M. Sprague, Auburn.
Aids, S. W. Lane, Augusta; John W. Berry, Gardiner; Fred W. Plaisted, Augusta; A. B. Nealey, Lewiston.
National Home Band, Togus.
Col. J. J. Lynch and Staff.
Commanding Provisional Battalion of Infantry and
First Maine Battery as escort.
Pall Bearers.
Hearse.
Capital Guards as Guard of Honor.

Carriages containing family and relatives, Governor Marble and staff, Governors of other States and staffs, Executive Councillors, Judiciary, Brigadier General Mitchell and Staff, State Officers, Legislative Committee, United States Officials and resident Clergymen.

Members and ex-members of the Legislature, Representatives of City Governments, delegations from various organizations, and citizens, on foot.

Private carriages.

During the services at the State House the Governor's salute will be fired from the United States Arsenal. Minute guns will be fired from the State grounds by a detail from the United States Arsenal under the direction of Capt. Michaelis, and the bells of Augusta and Hallowell will be tolled during the march from the State House to the cemetery.

On arrival at the cemetery the usual military and civic honors will be paid. At the close of the services a salvo of artillery and the Governor's salute will be fired from the State grounds.

Guns will be fired from the United States Arsenal every half-hour from sunrise to sunset.

Delegations from out of town are requested to report to the chief of staff at the State pension office.

By order of
GEORGE D. BISBEE,
Chief Marshal.

HENRY M. SPRAGUE,
Chief of Staff.

THE STATE FUNERAL.

The decorators completed their work Monday, and everything was in order for the solemn occasion. Additional festoons were hung upon the sides of the Council Chamber, the Governor's Room and Representatives' Hall, of broad streamers of black crape and white thibet. The floral tributes were original, varied and beautiful. The designs were expressive, and the flowers composing them were brought from the best New England conservatories. The air of the somber rotunda was heavy with their fragrance. At the foot of the casket was a basket filled with beautiful hot-house flowers, the offering of the Governor and Council, the Military Staff and the Heads of Departments. On the north side of the rotunda, beneath the crayon portrait of the late Governor, was a large stand heavily draped in mourning, upon which other floral tributes were placed. First was a beautiful bible from the family relatives. It rested upon a bank of ferns and ivy leaves, and worked in amid the white flowers of the cover, were the dates 1818—1887, in immortelles. Next was the design from the employes of the Hallowell Granite Company, a monument of white flowers, pinks, roses and other flowers, around which was a wreath of flowers, and the whole trimmed with a fringe of smilax. The Governor's Staff also furnished a beautiful floral cross, the back and margin of which was composed of ivy leaves and white ferns. The front was made up of magnificent white flowers—Marechal Niel and Catherine Mermet roses, Roman Hyacinths and other handsome varieties. Over the arm of this cross was a floral sickle, the blade of which was made of carnation pinks of the same tint as the Catherine Mermet roses. The handle of this was made of green English ivy leaves. It was a beautiful and touching tribute. Two other designs were a beautiful floral pillow and an inclined wreath. The former was made of flowers, and bore the name of the Governor, composed of purple immortelles upon a white back ground. The wreath stood upon a bank of flowers as a base, and was composed of calla lilies, violets and rosebuds. A beautiful column four feet high, broken at the top, the shaft composed of white pinks and white roses, the base of delicate pink roses combined with maiden-hair ferns and English ivy, was the offering of the Bodwell Granite Company of Vinalhaven. A tribute from the Rockland Knights of Labor, consisted of a shield in the emblem of the K. of L., a circle containing a triangle in roses, with the inscription, "Our Employer," in immortelles above it.

Tuesday morning quite early, the crowds began to gather about the State House and many thousands were there during the day. The funeral services were held in Representatives' Hall and were solemn and imposing. The Hall was crowded to its utmost capacity, and only a small portion of those present could gain admission. Delegations came from all the large cities, and among those present in the Hall, were distinguished men from all parts of the State. At eleven o'clock the family and relatives came in, and following, the Governor and other State officials, the joint legislative special committee, the city committees, and delegations from various organizations throughout the State. Ex-Governors Perham, Plaisted and Robie were among those present. Rev. A. F. Skeele of Augusta opened the exercises by reading selections from the scriptures and then offered prayer. The Chickering Quartette of Augusta, assisted by Mrs. Fannie Milliken rendered a selection, when the funeral address was spoken by Rev. C. A. Hayden, Pastor of the Universalist Church in Auburn.

REV. MR. HAYDEN'S ADDRESS.

God has a great Bible and the lives of men are texts in it. "What is excellent as God lives is permanent."

It is my sad duty and privilege as well to try to do what some of you could do much better, voice the common sorrow of our State and country in the loss of one of our noblest and best citizens. What can I say more when all the masters of speech have preceded me? The press have done justice to his name, worth and work. They have marshaled their stately sentences, and all over this country the words of deserved and sincere eulogy have been scattered broadcast. It is not necessary, even if I were able, to go over the ground which has been covered so completely and so well and which is so familiar to you all. It is better that I should call attention to the qualities of manhood in our friend which made him what he was in all the places in life which he was called upon to take and which he filled so nobly. So in passing. I shall only briefly outline his business and professional career, leaving to others to do the work more fully and better, as should be done, in some permanent form, as an inspiration to our youth in the attainment of success without the sacrifice of moral principle; for his is a life worthy the study of every young man. He said in an after-dinner talk at Westbrook Commencement, last June, to the young men: "In your pursuit of honor or wealth or position, never accept them if in doing so you have to sacrifice your integrity." He had a right to utter such words, because they were eminently true of him.

Joseph R. Bodwell, born in Methuen, Massachusetts, in 1818, was early thrown on his own resources, and learned his trade when apprenticeship meant three years of steady, persistent application. He also labored on a farm for wages that would seem pitably small in these days. But those years of work and study seem to have been best fitted to prepare him for the real work of life and secure the remarkable success that came in later years. He was reading, working, studying all the time. His success was not that of luck, but by persistent energy and ability, and by honesty and labor did he achieve his success. He had the rare faculty of grasping all the details of every undertaking and discerning the outcome. He had oversight of all his vast business operations, every detail of which was well defined in his thought. One of the papers politically opposed to him said, and it is doubtless true, that "he knew exactly what every man in his employ ought to be asked to do, and it is but simple justice to the dead to say that he asked no more than that of any man." This is high praise, but well deserved, as we all believe; for he was in the best sense the laboring man's friend. He, the greatest worker among them all, knew how to sympathize with and help his employes. I think it is true that he did as much to develop the resources of our State as any one man has ever done. All the varied interests of the State were encouraged and helped by him; not only the granite business, but agriculture, manufactures, railroads, in fact, every enterprise that tended to the material advancement of the people, received substantial aid from his preeminent business ability.

In his political career he has shown the same sterling qualities that have distinguished him in other walks of life. He did not seek office. On the contrary, he said he had enough to do without that, and I think we are beginning to feel that he spoke truly, and that it was almost unkind to thrust this added labor upon him. He, however, served in the Legislature and was mayor of his own city, forwarding their interests with that fidelity, characteristic of the man in whatever he undertook. He never desired the office of Governor. It was urged upon him, and in order to gratify his friends and serve the State, he finally consented. Notwithstanding his vast business concerns, requiring as it would seem all his thought and time, in the executive chair he gave the needed attention to the just administration of the government of the State and took an interest in all the affairs concerning the welfare of the entire people.

He was a good governor. Is it too much for me to say that he was one of our best governors in this commonwealth? I do not say he never made a mistake or erred in judgment. To argue this would be to claim more than any human being can fulfil. I do claim that he tried conscientiously to do his duty and the right. On the temperance question he took a decided stand and insisted that the law should be enforced, and if officials did not do their duty, on receiving evidence to that effect he would remove them. His position on this question has been of great value to the cause. It is so regarded by earnest temperance workers, and his death is sincerely mourned by all temperance organizations in the State.

In social life the special charm of his character was revealed. He had a kind word for everybody. The children felt free with him as with a friend. His greeting was cordial, sincere and tender. Though filled with business cares and interests, he could engage even with children in the joy and the simplicity of their life. His little grandson was his pride and delight. It was my privilege ten years ago to know something of his home life, and since that time I have seen him often; and he was always the kind, friendly, helpful man. In his home he laid aside perplexing business cares and entered into the pleasures and enjoyments of his guests with his family. A cordial, genial, modest man was he,—a kind and indulgent father, a considerate and affectionate husband. How many young men he has helped to succeed! What acts of charity continually flowed from his open hand! The best evidence of his worth is found in the universal sorrow seen and expressed by the citizens of his own city. The evidence of his liberality and justice to his workmen are found in their sad hearts and tearful faces. He was trusted and loved by them all.

He wrought, we say, *in stone*, and all over our land in most of our cities, are buildings and monuments showing the strength and extent of his business life. But his greatest achievement was in the building of his character, for the man was greater than his work. Behind all his achievements, behind all his successes stood the grand noble character which we mourn and which we admire this day. They said of him: "He is making his fortune," and that they all could see. That they praised, and said: "He is an industrious and excellent business man and is growing rich." I respect all that for what it is worth. But behind his fortune there was rising his character, stone upon stone, brick upon brick, story after story; for the man behind the work is what counts. After sixty-nine years of effort the work was accomplished, and the great Angel Death came and removed the scaffolding and revealed the completed manhood. We say prematurely, we regret that he was taken away—that all these interests will suffer in our State because he is no more. That, I grant you, is true. We shall miss him everywhere.

But there is another thought that comes in. Governor Bodwell stood on the summit, and when he passed on we can truly trust that God knew what was best. It is something to have lived sixty-nine years and commanded the respect and reverence of a whole country. It is a great thing to have lived and had the affection and sympathy of so dear friends and to hold so honored a place in human hearts. I am not sure but that it was his best time to go. With unimpaired faculties, amid prosperity, in the full vigor and maturity of his manhood, he has gone to his reward.

Governor Bodwell wielded a great influence in this community and wherever he was known. What is the explanation of this fact? By virtue of what quality did his opinion always command respect? What drew to him the many who from all classes and in all straits of life sought his counsel? Was it that his experience and training fitted him to speak with authority on most practical questions? Undoubtedly it was this coupled with a deeper fact, for his was not a limited culture of mere intellectual proficiency. His whole nature was broadly based on a moral or religious sense, and this is the prominent fact in the man's life. His intellect, his affections and desires, while they lacked nothing of power in themselves, were always subject to his feelings of duty. The degree in which conscience found expression through whatever he said or did gave him a very rare and remarkable manhood.

Joseph R. Bodwell was what he seemed to be. One might safely challenge any person to say that a closer acquaintance with him ever resulted in disappointment. No one ever penetrated behind an appearance in his life to find emptiness and unreality. Most people reveal weaknesses to their friends of which the world does not suspect them; but I am told by those who have known him intimately from his earliest years that this man exposed no more faults to those immediately about him than to the eye of society—a generous, christian gentleman.

The manhood of Governor Bodwell was genuine at every point. So thoroughly real and good in its strength, there was needed something more than a business or partial acquaintance with him to appreciate it. His earthly house, so full of life and purpose a few days ago, now lies here in state, idle and silent. But there does stand resting on the rock of ages, and reaching far up into the heavens, the great, brave character which the man has built in the everlasting sunlight of God, itself as everlasting and always as fair. This, his noblest work, will endure forever.

His charity was as unostentatious as the dew of summer, blessing the giver by the motive and the receiver by the quicker life and truer growth in human brotherhood. Even the daily press never accused his charity of being done for public notice and praise. A man of good judgment, good common sense, careful, exact, methodical, diligent. As regards the greater faculties of conscience and affection, the religious element, he possessed them all in a marked degree. He was well born, well bred, eminently well disciplined by himself. He was temperate in all his habits, never using liquor in any form or in any way. So by theory and practice he set an example of sobriety to us all. Learning to economize early in life, he laid the foundation for his fortune in the habits of economy, probity and honesty which marked him as the upright man and citizen whom thousands rise up to honor this day. Here was a man who knew the difference between the means of living and the true ends of life. He knew the true use of riches. They served as a material basis for great manly excellence. His use of money was a power to make those dear to him happy—to feed, to clothe, to house and warm and comfort needy men; to open avenues for the development of power and labor everywhere so that it might be a means of wealth to others. It was a means to educate the mind, to cheer the affections and bless the soul. It can be said of him as truly as was said of one of New England's great philanthropists: "To many a poor boy, to many a sad mother, he gave a merry Christmas on the earth; and now in good time God has taken him to celebrate Christmas and New Year's day in heaven."

Is it necessary, after all this has been manifested in so many ways by people of all shades of opinion, by testimony from all sources, in the sorrow in his own city and State, to say that Joseph R. Bodwell was a deeply religious man? All those traits of character constitute a Christian. If they do not, so much the worse for Christianity. More and more we are testing a man's piety, not by what he says, but by his deeds. "By their fruits ye shall know them." Not profession but character is the test. And I know of no man who could better stand that test. And when we have said that a man was honest, just and loving, conscientious and faithful in all the relations of life, we have said he was truly religious.

There are some, of whom when they die it is thought forcible praise to say that they had no religion to speak of, meaning, I suppose, that their religion was too vital, too real and deep to be spoken of. So far as this might also mean that religion is a thing not of words but of life, it might with perfect truth be said of our friend. But I am not satisfied with that kind of expression. I do not fear to say of him: "He had religion to speak of, though he rarely spoke of it himself, and never by way of asserting any merit of his own. Yet he was a firm believer and a constant doer in the work of the Gospel, in our church and denomination. He was interested in our schools, being on the board of trustees of Westbrook Seminary, and a liberal giver for all our work. But he did not confine his generosity to his own sect. I do not stand here to-day to claim him as a partisan in any particular way. He belonged to us all. He belonged to the State and all its interests were his interest, and whatever appealed to his nobler nature and to the instincts of his generosity was freely and gladly helped, though the appeal came from those with whom he differed.

I do not think he cared much for theology or dogmas of any kind. I never discussed with him questions of theology. There did not seem to be time. The hours were so few that the minister could spend with him. His mind seemed to me always to go in the direction of social and humane concerns from which it were poor appreciation to divert it for the sake of mere intellectual comparisons. I always noticed that preaching drew his

3

warmest sympathy which presented the kindly, tender, trustful, cheerful views of life and conduct. Whatever came to a practical bearing upon men and affairs seemed to win at once his sympathy. His face would light up and he would give encouragement to his minister by showing that he was heartily in earnest and interested in the presentation of anything concerning the good of humanity.

But whatever belief he held and whatever he rejected, his religion was his life and his life was his religion,—a living epistle known and read of all men. This being true, nothing could add to it or take from it. When I say he was a religious man I mean that he loved God and loved man. He had no more doubt that God would save and bless him and all men than that he himself would make all men happy if he could. Reverencing God, he reverenced the laws of God,—morality, justice and love. His religion was not stern and forbidding. His piety became morality, and a good deal more than that. He said the evening before he died that he was on the up-grade, meaning on the road to health. May we not in this presence to day, surrounded by these tokens of mourning, give a higher significance to the words now? He has always been on the up-grade from the very first start in life, humble though it was, working his way steadily up, never sacrificing principle or integrity for success, but always laying the foundation broadly for the growth of his character. It has been up-grade and a steep grade for him many times, yet never did he falter, but he went steadily on with that summit in sight which he was determined to reach at the last. In all the affairs of life, in which we knew him, can we not say of him truly: This man was a man on the up-grade in the best sense of the word; the rarest product of our New England life and character, a man to honor, a man to love, a man who could draw out the feelings and sympathies of those who knew him, and yet make them feel better for having known him? I could ask, I presume, in this presence to-day, these men who have met him in the official line of life, whether they looked upon him simply as the head of the State and as a man who outranked them in his position, or rather as a personal friend. I could ask them if, when they were in his presence, he did not impress them as a man that they were free to approach, a man who had gained the sympathy and love and respect which outpours itself in this generous expression throughout our State to-day?

He had the upward look, and, believing in all that was best, moved on toward their consummation. So his life climbed to the heights of morality and spiritual attainment, reaching at last, it seems to me, the summit on earth; and if it was up-grade at the last moment, it was because the air of earth had become too dense for him, and his struggling soul looked up to breathe the clearer and purer air of heaven; and when that great friend of us all said to him, "Friend, come up higher," he was ready and entered into rest.

Have you ever known what it is to look across the desolate night of sorrow and bereavement, seeing nothing? And have you cried out: "I shall see him but not now. I shall behold him, but not nigh?" That is how the hungry, longing, bereaved spirit always feels. I may see him, but not now. In the far off future when God's Angel comes with his dusky wings and gathers away, all too soon, some that we love and takes them through the portal of death, it is because our eyes are holden that we do not see him to be God's messenger. Death is the bell of evening telling the over-tired laborer that it is time to go home. His work on earth was done. His life has really just begun, and through the hope of the Resurrection, through the portals of that larger and that better life he has not stopped as we think, but has gone on and will go on to shine among the stars in heaven. He will show that those traits of character which made him what he was here, shine more resplendent when mortality has put on immortality and when that which was sown in weakness was raised into power. Oh, if we could be wise enough then to say: "I shall see him, but not now. I shall behold him, but not nigh." Then it would be light at eventide.

And now, friends, this so inadequate yet sincere testimony is from one who knew and loved him. With a little poem of Whittier, whom he loved and we all love, I will close this address:

"He has done the work of a true man,
  Crown him, honor him, love him,
Weep over him tears of woman,
  Stoop manliest brows above him.

For the warmest of hearts is frozen,
  The freest of hands is still,
And the gap in our picked and chosen
  The long years may not fill.

No duty could overtask him,
  No need his will outrun,
Or ever our lips could ask him
  His hands the work had done.

He forgot his own soul for others,
  Himself to his neighbor lending,
He found the Lord in his suffering brothers,
  And not in the clouds descending.

Ah, well, the world is discreet,
  There are plenty to pause and wait,
But here was a man who set his feet
  Sometimes in advance of fate.

Never rode to the wrong's redressing
  A worthier paladin;
Shall he not hear the blessing,
  "Good and faithful enter in"?

"DUST TO DUST."

There was a death-like stillness in the Hall during the delivery of the address, and at its close another selection was sung by the Quartette. It was a finely executed number and thrilled the large audience. The benediction was pronounced by the Rev. J. S. Gledhill, which closed the funeral exercises. The rotunda was cleared, and the family were given an opportunity to take a last look and final farewell of him who had been so much beloved by them all.

The procession was formed by Marshal Bisbee and his aids. At one o'clock, the military escort, which had formed on Water Street, marched to the State House and was drawn up in double file, facing it. The order of procession was as follows:

Platoon of Police.
Chief Marshal and Aids—Hon. Geo. D. Bisbee of Buckfield, Chief Marshal; Col. H. M. Sprague of Auburn, Chief of Staff; Capt. S. W. Lane of Augusta, Maj. John W. Berry of Gardiner, Fred W. Plaisted of Augusta. Col. A. B. Nealey of Lewiston.
National Home Band, Togus.
Col. John J. Lynch and Staff commanding the provisional Battalion of Infantry, and the First Maine Battery as escort.
Pall Bearers.
Hon. Hannibal Hamlin. Bangor; Hon. D. F. Davis, Bangor; Hon. H. M. Plaisted, Augusta; Hon. Frederick Robie, Gorham; Hon. Albion Little, Portland; Hon. John S. Case, Rockland; Hon. John M. Adams, Deering; Col. Mark F. Wentworth, Kittery; Hon. James H. Leigh, Hallowell.
Hearse.
Capital Guards as Guard of Honor.
Carriages containing the family and immediate relatives.
Gov. Marble and Staff, Ex-Governor Perham, Governors of Other States and Staffs, Executive Council Judiciary, Brigadier-General Mitchell and staff, State Officers, Legislative Committee, United States Officers and Resident Clergymen.
Representatives of City Government, delegations from various organizations and citizens on foot.
Private Carriages.

The military organizations and procession battalion forming the escort were as follows :

FIELD AND STAFF 1ST REGIMENT, M. V. M.

Col. John J. Lynch of Portland, Commanding.
Lieut. Col. E. H. Ballard, Augusta.
Major B. J. Hill, Auburn.
Adjutant Edward E. Philbrook, Portland.
Surgeon, Major George H. Brickett, Augusta.

FROM 1ST REGIMENT.

Company A. (Portland Light Infantry) Capt. Benj. A. Norton.
Company B. (Portland Mechanic Blues) Capt. Chas. W. Davis.
Company C. (Auburn Light Infantry) Capt. Fred H. Storah.
Company E. (Montgomery Guards, Portland) Capt. Timothy E. Hartnett.

SECOND REGIMENT.

Company D. (Nealey Rifles, Lewiston) Capt. Walter A. Goss.
Company E. (Skowhegan Light Infantry) Capt. Horace M. Weston.
Company G. (Hamlin Rifles, Bangor) Capt. L. S. Chilcott.
Company H. (Waterville Light Infantry) Capt. William Vaughan.

FIRST MAINE BATTERY, Brunswick—Capt. O. T. Despeaux, Commanding.

First Platoon, Lewiston—Lieut. M. J. Moriarty.
Second Platoon, Brunswick—Lieut. Isaac N. Frink.

GUARD OF HONOR—1st Reg't, M. V. M.

Company F. (Capital Guards, Augusta) Capt. Winfield S. Choate.

The funeral march, called "Governor Bodwell's Funeral March," was composed for the occasion by Prof. B. W. Thieme of the National Home Band.

Governor Ames of Massachusetts was represented by Adjutant General Dalton, and others of his staff.

There was a touching scene in the rotunda before the removal of the casket. The children of the Bath Orphan's Home, twelve in number, placed upon it a floral tribute of cut flowers which was very beautiful, also a card which read as follows:

"In grateful remembrance of the kindness shown by our departed Governor to the children of the Bath Military and Naval Orphan Home on their recent visit to the capitol, this simple offering is made."

The Augusta Capital Guards, Captain W. S. Choate commanding, marched in the procession as a guard of honor. The soldierly bearing of the detachment from this company while on duty at the State House was highly commended by all. The signal gun for the procession to move was fired a few minutes before two o'clock. The column was at once set in motion, while at intervals, minute guns were fired at the grounds of the capitol. Arrived at the Hallowell cemetery, the casket was gently taken from the hearse and placed in its final resting place. Then above the oppressive stillness, came the mighty crash of artillery, as three salvos were fired from the guns of the regular battery belonging to the Kennebec Arsenal, and the funeral services were over.

There was grief in every heart and tears in many eyes, as the vast concourse of people which had gathered at the cemetery turned away and started homeward, and a feeling was manifest that they had indeed taken a final leave of all that was mortal of their late Governor and friend.

The following resolves were passed by the Executive Council:

'In Council,
December 20, 1887. }

WHEREAS. It has pleased Almighty God to remove from our midst the Chief Magistrate of our State, Joseph R. Bodwell, therefore,

Resolved, That in his sudden and untimely death the State of Maine has not only lost a most able, conscientious and upright Executive, but that we, as members of his Council, feel deeply the loss of a personal friend, and who in all his walk and conversation impressed us with the great worth of his character and it is with unqualified pleasure that we bear testimony that in his short official life with us his only aim and purpose was to do right.

Resolved, That the members of the Executive Council wear a badge of mourning upon the left breast for thirty days, and that all State officials be requested to do the same.

Resolved, That these Resolutions be spread upon the Records of the Council and a copy be engrossed and forwarded to the family.

Read and unanimously adopted.

ORAMANDAL SMITH,
Secretary of State.

IN COUNCIL, }
December 20, 1887. }

WHEREAS, The Governor and Council desire to express their appreciation of assistance rendered them in the discharge of the sorrowful duty of arranging for the funeral of our late Governor, Joseph R. Bodwell, therefore,

Resolved, That a vote of thanks be and is hereby extended to Councillor Seth M. Carter, Judge George C. Wing and General George L. Beal, the committee of arrangements ; to the Hon. George D. Bisbee, chief marshal; to his aids. Col. Henry M. Sprague, chief of staff, Capt. S. W. Lane, Major John W. Berry. Fred W. Plaisted and Col. A. B. Nealey ; to Mayor George E. Macomber, chairman, and the other gentlemen comprising the general reception committee ;* to A. M. Spear, Esq., and Hon. William D. Pennell, chief ushers, for the prompt and efficient service they have rendered ; to Rev. Charles A. Hayden and other officiating clergymen ; to the Chickering quartette, with Mrs. Milliken, for the able and appropriate conduct of the ceremonies ; to Gen. Luther Stephenson, Jr., of the National Soldiers' Home, and to Capt. Michaelis of the United States Arsenal for their kind tender of the band and battery ; to Capt. W. S. Choate and the Capital Guards, and other officers and men of the military for the part they have taken ; to Mr. Payson Tucker, general manager of the Maine Central Railroad, for the ample accommodations and transportation provided, and to the many citizens who so kindly furnished us with every facility, and rendered us every service in their power.

The Legislative Committee was constituted as follows : S. H. Allen, A. W. Rich, George P. Wescott and Samuel Libby of the Senate; and Chas. E. Littlefield, J. H Manley, F. A. Powers, Fred N. Dow, J. C. Talbot, Lewis A. Barker, E. L. Pattangall and E. K. O'Brien of the House.

---

*Besides Mayor Macomber, the reception committee was composed as follows : Geo. E. Weeks, E. C. Allen, Chas. E. Nash, H. M. Heath, L. C. Cornish, Thomas Lombard, C. W. Whitten, M. V. B. Chase, S. Titcomb, Elias Milliken, P. O. Vickery and Ira H. Randall.

Bodwells of Methuen.

The Bodwells have ever been prominent in the town of Methuen. At the incorporation of the town in 1725, Daniel Bodwell was one of the selectmen. At the beginning of the Revolutionary war, two persons bearing the name of Bodwell were on the committee of correspondence and safety. Henry Bodwell, the first of the name in this country, was a soldier in Philip's Indian war and was wounded; he took the freeman's oath in Newbury in 1678, then aged 24 years. Where he was born, his civil condition, the date of his emigration and the place where he landed on American soil, are alike unknown at this date. May 4, 1681, he married Bethiah, daughter of John, Jr., and Mary (Webster) Emery of Newbury. He lived a short time in Newbury, his oldest child, Bethiah, being born there in 1682, and then moved to Andover, where he was living in 1685. In 1693, John Emery of Newbury gave to his daughter Bethiah, and her husband Henry Bodwell, one hundred acres of land situated in Haverhill. In 1712, he was living in Haverhill. He was a renowned hunter and marksman, and a terror to the hostile Indians. He is said, on one occasion, to have shot an Indian on the opposite side of the Merrimack, who, thinking himself at a safe distance off, was making insulting gestures. Bodwell's Ferry and also Bodwell's Falls, commemorate the name of Henry Bodwell. The children of Henry and Bethiah Bodwell were as follows:

I. *Bethiah*, b. June 2, 1682.
II. *Mary*, b. April 1,1684.
III. *Henry* and *Josiah*, (twins) b. January 27, 1685—both d. same year.
IV. *Abigail*, b. January 15, 1686.
V. *Henry*, b. November 6, 1688.
VI. *James*, b. January 16, 1691.
VII. *Daniel*, b. February 14, 1693.
VIII. *Sarah*, b. December 1, 1694.
IX. *Hannah*, b. September 1, 1696.
X. *Judith*, b. April 4, 1698.
XI. *Ruth*, b. December 2, 1699.

Henry Bodwell, Jr., married in 1726, Ann, and had the following children:

I. *Ann*, b. February 25, 1727.
II. *Henry*, b. July 26, 1729; m. Mary Robinson.*
III. *Phebe*, b. February 15, 1731.
IV. *Bethiah*, b. May 25, 1734.
V. *Joshua*, b. October 4, 1736.
VI. *Mary*, b. July 21. 1740.
VII. *William*, b. March. 1743; d. young.
VIII. *William*, b. May 18, 1747.

HENRY, above-named, who married Mary, daughter of Joseph Robinson of Haverhill, afterwards of Roxford, had the following children:

I. *Henry*, b. January 8. 1762.
II. *Isaac*, b. October 16. 1765.
III. *Olive*, b. October 15, 1767.
IV. *Persis*, b. July 30, 1769.
V. *Joseph*, b. November 2, 1771; m. Mary How.
VI. *Nathan*, b. October 12, 1773.
VII. *Arnold*, b. March 22. 1776.
VIII. *Elizabeth*, b. June 24, 1778.

JOSEPH BODWELL, the fifth child of Henry and Mary (Robinson) Bodwell, lived in that part of Methuen which has since been set off and incorporated as Lawrence. He occupied the homestead of his father, and engaged in farming, teaming and in other pursuits. His children were:

I. *Mary*, b. September 15, 1796; m. Patrick Flemming.
II. *Nathan*, b. September 23, 1798.
III. *Joseph Robinson*, b. October 18, 1800; d. young.
IV. *Hazen*, b. May 26, 1803.
V. *Hannah*, b. June 9, 1807.
VI. *Christopher*, b. October 14, 1809.
VII. *Persis*, b. November 23, 1811.
VIII. *Elizabeth*, b. February 22, 1814.
IX. *Nancy*, b. March 16, 1816.
X. *Joseph Robinson*, (Governor Bodwell) b. June 18. 1818.
XI. *Henry A.*, b. August 27. 1821.

JOSEPH R. BODWELL, the tenth child of Joseph and Mary (How) Bodwell, married first, October 3, 1848, Eunice, daughter of Josiah and Hannah (Austin) Fox of Dracut, Mass. She was born October 22, 1822, and died in Methuen. December 14, 1857. He married, second, July 25, 1859. Hannah C. Fox, sister of his first wife, who was born in Dracut, August 3, 1825. Children:

I. *Persis Mary*, b. August 26, 1849; m. January 2, 1871, Rev. Jotham M. Paine, who died September 19, 1880, and had Charlie Bodwell (Paine), b. May 28, 1873.
II. *Joseph Fox*, b. July 11, 1862.

*Born August 3, 1737, daughter of Joseph and Mehitable (Eames) Robinson, granddaughter of Joseph and Sarah (Stevens) Robinson, and great granddaughter of Joseph Robinson, born 1644-5, married May 30, 1671, Elizabeth Ingalls Dane of Andover, Mass. Governor Bodwell was named for his Robinson ancestors.

Tribute of the Press.

HALLOWELL REGISTER. The grief over Governor Bodwell's death is deep and sincere. There are not many homes in Hallowell where his generosity has not shown liberal work; and the whole community, not one family, is in mourning for their honored dead. The loss financially cannot be estimated. Governor Bodwell was Hallowell's best friend as well as her most distinguished citizen. His business sagacity formed the strong foundation for the immense granite works of the city; he was interested in all public enterprises. As a philanthropist, his heart was big enough to take in all men of all ranks.

Mr. Bodwell is best known as a business man. He was reluctant to accept honors at the hands of his fellow citizens, who would have delighted to have continued him in the most responsible places in their gift. Still he was twice made mayor of the city, declining re-election for the third term; twice made representative to the State Legislature; twice did Maine Republicans send him to their national convention; and he was finally chosen by the people to the highest office in their gift. All unite in warmest praise of his administration. Earnest men and women, the whole State over, believed in him and endorsed his efforts to gain the enforcement of all the laws. His death is well-nigh a calamitous blow to the governmental as well as business interests of the State.

KENNEBEC JOURNAL. This unexpected and melancholy event produces a deep sensation throughout the State and in other sections of the country where he was well known. A man of very superior capacity, of great energy and executive ability, the architect of his own fortune, his large business enterprises have employed capital and labor on a broad scale. Starting from humble circumstances, he had by his force of character become recognized as one of the leading personalities of the State, one of the foremost men of New England. Of large hearted generosity, faithful in the performance of private and public duties, a devoted husband and father, a noble citizen, his death is an irreparable loss to his family, to his large number of friends and to Maine, whose honored Chief Magistrate he has proved himself during a year of successful administration.

4

GOSPEL BANNER. As a citizen Governor Bodwell was as exemplary and influential as in his diversified business transactions. As Mayor, legislator, political adviser, and Governor, he was straightforward and upright, performing every duty faithfully and unselfishly. These virtues characterized his whole life, indeed. At home, in society, in business circles, in official station, he was ever the same honest, unassuming, conscientious, capable man.

Accepting the doctrines of Universalism as the truth divinely communicated to man, his life was an illustration of the faith he held, that God is the universal Father and all men are brethren. His naturally sympathetic nature, his cheerful, genial, patient disposition, were strengthened by his cheering and satisfying religious views. In all the years of his business career he had the good-will of his many workmen because he sought ever to do by them as he would have an employer do by him. The Golden Rule was the chief principle in his system of political economy. That never fails to beget confidence, respect and loyalty toward a capitalist who practices it in his dealings with a few or many workmen.

MAINE FARMER. His character and purpose partook of the solidity of the blocks of granite from his quarries in the hillsides, becoming beautiful and symmetrical as these same blocks of granite after passing under the hammer and the chiselling strokes of the artist. He was especially the friend of the laboring man, because he had been with him in all his experience, shared with him his humble fare, and patiently and manfully toiled to attain the position in life which patient toil and true worth will bring. He knew how to sympathize with the laboring man, because his great mind grasped readily the problems of business. He initiated new enterprises, involving a large expenditure of labor and capital. He would weigh well the chances of success, organize the enterprise and set the wheels in motion; and death found his hands and brain full of schemes for expanding the business and developing the resources of the State of his adoption,—the State which he had honored in citizenship, and which in turn had conferred upon him its highest honors. He was an approachable man, hampered by no superficial ideas of false dignity; warm and cordial in his greetings to his friends. He was always frank, free, courteous, generous, manly. In his brief official career as Governor, he brought to the office the same characteristics that were so conspicuous in private. He did not weigh for a moment what effect his acts would have upon himself or his party; his only inquiry was whether it was legally and morally right, and whether it would be of benefit to the people at large. And when fully convinced that the measure was right, he would be as firm and unyielding as his own granite hills. He was an intense American, the ripe, rich product of our hardy New England civilization and institutions. His life and toilsome progress up the hill of success will be a constant inspiration to the young man, struggling on the farm, in the shop, in the mill, at the work bench, in the quarries. In the death of Governor Bodwell, the State is bereft of the services of a faithful Chief

Magistrate, the cause of temperance of one of its most consistent upholders, the town of his residence one of its most enterprising citizens, his workmen of a just and considerate employer, and his family of a kind husband and father.

NEW AGE. What was there in this man's life to call forth so much of general public sympathy and sorrow, and what the lesson and moral of it all? It was the great and good qualities of his head and heart as a business man, that made him so esteemed in life and so regretted in death.

He was Governor, but that added nothing to the public regret—except the regret that he should have been persuaded to accept the position. "In the light of events," as Mr. Hayden said, "it must seem something more than unkind to force upon him that responsibility. He had business enough." He was a rich man, so esteemed, but he was no more honored for his wealth than envied for it. Men have died in our midst leaving millions and had no mourners—not one, because their money-making was without one generous purpose, without a thought of the public good, of the general welfare; promoting no industries, engaging in no business but that of the miser—only hoarding, and they had their reward.

It was the use Mr. Bodwell made of his wealth as a business man, in promoting the industries of the State, that causes him to be lamented and honored. If he desired to make money, it was because he loved to do business—the more money and credit at his command, the more business, the development of more industries, and the helping of more men to help themselves. Animated by these generous purposes, his benevolence did not contract, only expanded, with his means, having no more of the miser in his composition than Santa Claus. It was this large-hearted and whole-souled man, and public spirited citizen, Joseph R. Bodwell, whose death is so generally and deeply felt, and whose memory is so honored. The lessons of his life are many and the moral of it plain.

EASTERN FARMER. In the death of Governor Bodwell, Maine sustains the greatest loss it ever experienced in the decease of one man. As an executive officer, Governor Bodwell has proved what his most intimate friends expected he would, viz., one of the most successful and popular of Maine's popular Governors. He entered upon the unsought office with that honesty of purpose that has characterized his entire life, to administer the laws of the State with equity and justice. The will of the people, so far as he understood it, has been his will.

As a business man Mr. Bodwell had few equals. Although his enterprises were enormous in magnitude and varied in their nature, his master mind could comprehend and direct them all. His judgment was proverbial, much sought and prized, whether it was in the construction of a State House, or the building of a railroad; whether it was lumbering, or the management of an enormous manufacturing establishment, of either wood or metals; whether it was farming or stock husbandry: with his wonderful business capacity he could grasp them all, and has proved their success beyond a doubt. It is in these great enterprises that Mr. Bodwell's removal will be most keenly felt by thousands of workmen who were directly employed, and thousands more indirectly in the business enterprises, the head and front of which was this one man.

WATERVILLE SENTINEL. It is estimated that at least ten thousand people passed through the rotunda of the State House during the day of the funeral. It was not an altogether formal tribute of mere respect to high station—a perfunctory duty to the memory of a Governor of the State. Indeed, such motive could not have called together such numbers from all ranks of life and all parties from every considerable town in the State. It was a deeper feeling. There was the sense of personal as well as public loss, and a sense of individual bereavement was felt by hundreds whose recollections of Joseph R. Bodwell will for many years verify the familiar couplet:

> The sweet remembrance of the just
> Shall flourish when he sleeps in dust.

KENNEBEC DEMOCRAT. In the death of Joseph R. Bodwell, Maine loses one of its best citizens, a man of great business capacity, who was largely interested in promoting enterprises that tended to the welfare and prosperity of the State. The press and people universally join in expressing their sympathy for the family of the deceased and pay a just tribute to the man, who by perseverance and honest toil, has risen from a poor boy to a condition of wealth and prominence.

PORTLAND PRESS. By the death of Governor Bodwell the State loses not only its executive head, but also a public spirited citizen who has created great enterprises which have been of great value to our people, and have contributed much to the prosperity of the State. Long before he became Governor Mr. Bodwell was known and respected throughout the State for his business capacity and success; for his interest in all good causes and his liberality in promoting them; for his simplicity and uprightness of character. He had seen little of public life when the people of Maine elected him to the governorship against his wish, almost against his protest. As the chief magistrate of the State his course has been distinguished by the same traits that characterized his career in private life. He has performed the duties that devolved upon him with care and conscientiousness, and with an eye single to the welfare of the State. Mistakes he may have made, but his general course has been one to commend him to the people of the State without distinction of party, as a thoroughly upright, faithful and conscientious public officer. Governor Bodwell was the architect of his own fortune, and his career is a conspicuous illustration of the possibilities before the young man in a land where the avenues to success in life are open to every one on equal terms. What he was he made himself. He began the battle of life with no reliance but a clear head, a sound body and a correct moral sense, but industry and perseverance coupled with good judgment brought him wealth and honor. His

45

life was a noble one, noble in its aspirations and in its achievements, and the story of it should be an inspiration to every young man. His pathway at the outset was filled with discouragements, and there was little promise of the signal success he was destined to achieve. But he battled on until he had conquered them all and placed his name high up in the list of the honored men of his State. Against his name is now set the asterisk of death, but his memory will be cherished so long as men continue to admire a life of high aspiration, of noble achievement, of conscientious performance of duty.

EVENING EXPRESS. Governor Bodwell was emphatically one of the people. He was self-made, and achieved a high measure of success. The example of his life is one full of encouragement to the youth of our State, the hardy sons of toil, who have few advantages. He began his career with little save willing hands, a stout heart, and an integrity proof against all the blandishments of vice. Although unskilled in state-craft, he has filled the gubernatorial chair with dignity and strength and to the satisfaction of all good people.

In the death of Governor Bodwell, the State is bereft of the services of a faithful Chief Magistrate, the cause of temperance of one of its most consistent upholders, the town of his residence one of its most enterprising citizens, his workmen of a just and considerate employer, and his family of a kind husband and father.

Governor Bodwell was broad in his sympathies, generous and just in his nature, and the soul of integrity. He was a Republican in politics as the result of convictions strengthened by years of study and observation; but he was not a narrow man in any particular.

EASTERN ARGUS. Joseph R. Bodwell was a man of great force of character and unquestioned integrity. From humble beginnings he, by industry, frugality and sagacity, built up a great business in his adopted State, and came to be its executive. Kindly of heart and open of hand, he endeared himself to all those who had dealings with him. The most touching tribute of his worth is the grief of the men who knew him best—the men in his employ, who so often profited by his kindness, and whose fortunes he was always ready and often eager to advance.

PORTLAND ADVERTISER. Governor Bodwell was emphatically a self-made man. The story of his career illustrates anew the opportunities open to a poor boy in this country, and shows what may be accomplished on a capital of nothing but industry, perseverance and sound sense. Conscientiousness and good intentions have directed Governor Bodwell's executive acts, and his has been an administration of high respectability. He dies universally honored and regretted.

LEWISTON JOURNAL. The most profound sorrow will be caused throughout our State and wherever our good Governor was known among men, by the news of the death of Joseph R. Bodwell, the Chief

Magistrate of Maine. Governor Bodwell was esteemed for both his noble private life and his conscientious performance of his public duties. He was a sterling man and a sterling Governor. He was loved best at Hallowell, where he was loved as a neighbor and friend—the best friend that Hallowell ever had.

The story of Governor Bodwell's life is already well known to the people of Maine. It is the story of a boy who struggled against obstacles which would have dismayed a heart less stout than his, but who conquered and became one of the richest and most honored citizens of his adopted State. The secret of his success may be seen in his determined perseverance and in his unerring fidelity to his associates as well as to himself. If ever there was a true man, Governor Bodwell was one. If ever there was a man whom temptation could not lure from the line of rectitude and honor, Governor Bodwell was one. Recognizing his solid abilities, it is his firm and spotless character that we most admire.

When he was elected Governor of Maine, he had very little acquaintance with the affairs of the State, and it was a trying position for him; but he devoted his rugged and unbending energies to its demands, and proved in every way equal to them. It was very evident to all observers that Governor Bodwell was Governor of Maine, himself! His individuality was prominent in all his official acts. He performed every duty as his conscience directed. He was a strong Governor. His vigorous efforts to have all the laws of the State enforced made the conspicuous feature of his administration. His death will be especially deplored by the friends of law, order and temperance, in whose support his back-bone had proven a column of iron.

BANGOR WHIG AND COURIER. The sudden announcement of the death of Governor Bodwell just at a time when the people of Maine, after days of anxious watching, were beginning to feel a sense of security and to hope that our honored Chief Magistrate was on the road to a speedy recovery, will prove a severe shock to the entire State, which is thus deprived of a most worthy Executive as well as a highly esteemed and valued citizen. In the death of Governor Bodwell the State of Maine meets with a loss that cannot be overestimated, not so much on account of his official connection with the government, for, notwithstanding the unquestioned merit of his administration, strong and earnest as it was, his place as Chief Executive can be filled, but the place of Joseph R. Bodwell the public-spirited, broad-minded, energetic and whole-souled citizen cannot be supplied. Always ready to respond to the appeal for aid, and with the recollection of his own early struggles fresh in his memory, his sympathy and generous assistance were freely given to those who, like himself, had to make their own way in the world. He was a philanthropist in the full sense of the word and gave freely of his large means to aid all worthy objects. As Governor, the same devotion to principle that ever manifested itself in his private business relations marked his public career. He devoted his best energies to the promotion of the welfare of the State, always acting up to his true convictions in all his official acts. An honest, true man, his life in public as well as private affairs has been one of spotless integrity. A fearless champion of what he believed to be right, and an uncompromising foe to all wrong doing, he leaves a name that will long be honored in the State of his adoption.

BANGOR COMMERCIAL. It is not too much to say that the announcement of the death of Governor Joseph R. Bodwell, which occurred at his residence in Hallowell at an early hour this morning, will cause a more painful shock to the people of the State than the decease of perhaps any other eminent citizen would have done. This is not perhaps so much due to the exalted office which Mr. Bodwell held as to the feeling that he represented in himself the growing prosperity of the State, whose resources his tireless energy had done so much to develop.

Governor Bodwell always believed in the future of Maine, and his confidence was of that practical character which leads the possessor to invest money and time to aid in its realization. There was no branch of industrial development in Maine in which Governor Bodwell's business genius and tireless energy did not make itself felt. In agriculture, in manufacturing, in railroad development, in extensive business enterprises of all kinds, he has been constantly and extensively engaged and in all he has been successful. One great secret of his business success seems to have been his faculty of selecting the right men to co-operate with him and then in infusing into them a portion of his own enthusiasm in his work. He was a man of very decided convictions and could not be swerved from what he believed to be right by any considerations of mere expediency.

Personally Governor Bodwell was a most agreeable gentleman. He had a very kind heart and his charities have been numerous if not ostentatious in their character. His death will be deeply felt all over the State, and it is to be feared that to some of the extensive enterprises in which he was engaged his loss will be almost irreparable.

BIDDEFORD JOURNAL. To-day Maine mourns the loss of her Chief Magistrate and one of her foremost citizens. The click of the telegraph that announced the death of Joseph R. Bodwell at an early hour this morning, sent a shock over the State that was responded to with bowed heads and one universal utterance of sorrow and lamentation.

By this sudden dispensation of Providence, Maine loses a model citizen and a model Governor. At the time of his death his business relations were simply stupendous, reaching from Maine to Georgia, and embracing a wide variety of interests. But amid it all no cloud ever rose to obscure his rising sun. As the head of a household; as a neighbor, pure and above reproach in private life; as a man of honor and strict integrity in small and large business affairs alike, and as a shining example, from the small beginnings of early boyhood to the zenith of his wonderfully successful life, but few men in Maine or out of it to-day measure up to his full stature of excellence.

Less than a year ago he was inaugurated Governor. The people of Maine know his record. He has stamped his grand individuality upon his brief administration in characters of living light, which will give him an enduring place among Maine's ablest and best chief magistrates, and prove eminently worthy of emulation by those who may come after him.

CALAIS ADVERTISER. Governor Bodwell was emphatically a self-made man. The story of his career illustrates anew the opportunities open to a poor boy in this country, and shows what may be accomplished on a capital of nothing but industry, perseverance, and sound sense.

CAMDEN HERALD. An honest, courageous, noble man has fallen; and the expression of regret of men of all political parties is almost universal. His death, occurring so soon after his inauguration and just as the people of the State are learning his worth and ability as a ruler, is peculiarly sad.

REPUBLICAN JOURNAL. The story of Governor Bodwell's life is told in other columns. It is a record of which Americans may well feel proud, and conveys lessons that the young men of this country may study with profit. The farmer's boy, who, with no other capital than his strong muscles, stout heart, sterling integrity and sound common sense, attains wealth and high position, is a purely American product, and it is mainly to men of this stamp that the prestige and prosperity of our country are due. Maine owes to her late Governor a debt not readily computable. He was the pioneer and prime motor in the development of her granite industry. By the importation of blooded stock, and in other ways, he did much to promote our agricultural interests. He was concerned in Maine's winter harvest, the ice crop, and in building up our summer resorts. In short, he was a man of many and varied business interests—a man of rare executive ability and untiring industry. He was a friend of the educational interests, and so staunch a temperance man that in his last illness he positively refused to take stimulants.

Governor Bodwell was not a politician. In the few instances in which he held office the office sought the man, and was oftener refused than accepted. It was with great reluctance that he became a candidate for Governor last year, and it was only from a sense of duty to his party, for he was a staunch Republican, that he finally yielded to the solicitations of his friends. He brought to the office the same business methods followed in his private affairs, and sought to perform the duties in the interest of the whole people. No thought as to political consequences influenced his acts. An honest purpose characterized his administration. He was the friend of the working man, having never lost sight of his own early struggles, and the attainment of wealth and political honors made no change in his simple habits and unaffected manner of life. The many tributes to the memory of the deceased are well deserved, and he is sincerely mourned by all our people.

BELFAST CITY PRESS. Mr. Bodwell was, in many respects, a remarkable man and one of a type rarely found in any other country than ours, By his own native ability and unflagging energy he rose from poverty to wealth, from obscurity to become the governor of a State celebrated for producing able men. He brought to all his undertakings an earnestness of purpose which insured their success from the outset; he pushed them forward with a vigor which kept them constantly at the front. In all the varied relations of life he was an exemplary citizen. His reputation was unsullied, his disposition kindly, and his courage unflinching. His life has its lesson; so, too, has his death. That restless activity which impelled him forward from one enterprise to another, allowing him only the rest obtained from change of occupation, though one of the factors which rendered such a career possible, exacted its payment in so exhausting vitality as to occasion the sad event whereat an entire State mourns. Yet how better can a man die than in the flower of a well-spent life and at the topmost pinnacle of his success? In such a manner has our Chief Magistrate departed. May he rest in peace.

SOMERSET REPORTER. Sorrow for Governor Bodwell is genuine and pervades all classes. Probably no man in Maine was ever mourned more sincerely and generally. He was one of God's noblest works, "an honest man." His was a wonderful combination of soul, brain, energy. and courage such as appears only at the rarest intervals. One need only look into his honest eyes to know that the soul that looked out through them was a pure one, and that the brain behind them was a large, broad one. He drew his friends around him as with hooks of steel. Good men believed in him and stood by him when once they came to know him. His was a noble nature, and that nobility was manifested in unostentatious deeds of benevolence and charity. He was pre-eminently the laborer's friend, always popular with the hundreds of men constantly in his employ. He was a business man in its broadest sense, with a capacity to grasp the situation, comprehend great business problems and solve them. The loss to the State of so wise and faithful a chief magistrate is indeed great, but the loss to the business interests of the State is greater and second only to the loss sustained by his family friends. A great, a noble, a grand man is dead and the citizens of the State, without regard to party or creed, in every city, village and town mourn his decease.

AROOSTOOK TIMES. Governor Bodwell was honest and straightforward in all his dealings, and it is said of him that he could never understand or acquire the political diplomacy which shakes hands with and stabs a man at the same time. Having made up his mind that a measure was right and just, he gave it his support, and the political intrigue which surrounded him was uncongenial. His life furnishes an object lesson to the young of great value, showing, as it does, that there is no royal road

5

to fame and fortune in this land. It should serve to warn men like the late Governor that political preferment is an empty show and a sore vexation.

PISCATAQUIS OBSERVER. He was a powerful example of a self-made man. Born in obscurity, with an indomitable will and a determination to make something of himself, this giant fought his way, step by step, against odds that would terrify an ordinary heart. Liberal-minded, whole souled, with a capacity for business that was unlimited; fine social gifts, a big heart that went out toward his fellow men and melted at sight of suffering; always giving something for the needy; with love for truth, purity—yea, a Christianity that knew no creed, he was every inch a man; and his early death will be a great blow to State and Nation, and regretted by men of all parties or classes. He loved his State above the selfish clamor of party strife, and performed the duties of Chief Magistrate with a wisdom and impartiality born of his sagacity and noble character. But "the paths of glory lead but to the grave," and the good citizen, the tender-hearted, charitable man, the loving husband and father, is no more. Death claims its own, and the great man sleeps.

> "Leaves have their time to fall,
> And flowers to wither at the North-wind's breath,
> The stars to set;—but all,
> Thou hast all seasons for thine own, O Death!"

BOSTON TRAVELLER. He brought to the office of the Governorship a rare business experience and marked executive ability, and has honored his State as well as himself by his wise and vigorous administration of public affairs. Maine loses in his death an able executive, and one of the foremost and most public spirited of her citizens.

BOSTON HERALD. Governor Bodwell was not an orator or a politician. He was a plain, persistent busines man. He worked harder than any man in his employ, and he had many. His habits were simple, and he was not puffed up by money. When he ran for Governor, there were no scandals to be raked up for use against him. He was an excellent example of the best product of our institutions—honest, serviceable men.

BOSTON GLOBE. The death of Governor Bodwell of Maine is a surprise to the people of this State and elsewhere, though it was not wholly unexpected by those who were informed as to his condition. Governor Bodwell was a self-made man, and he endeavored to discharge faithfully the duties which the citizens of Maine committed to him.

BOSTON JOURNAL. Mr. Bodwell was generous in his impulses, affable in his manner, and in his private character without reproach. He was strictly temperate in practice as well as in theory, and the vigorous efforts which he made as Governor to secure the thorough enforcement of the liquor laws of the State were prompted by conviction, not by political exigency. He brought to the office of Governor the same qualities which had made his business career honorable and successful, and his administration reflects credit upon the State and honor upon his memory.

PROGRESSIVE AGE. He was a sample of the men who attain to conspicuous positions under our free government by unaided effort. In youth and early manhood, his lot was similar to tens of thousands who are deprived of adventitious aids to raise them to success. The way to riches and eminence which he travelled is open to every young man who has the native ability and capacity to success. Those are essential, and without them success is hardly attainable, struggle as we may. Those qualities joined to energetic, well directed labor were what secured to him an honorable position among the distinguished of the land. Of his social qualities as a man and a citizen, it is superfluous to speak.

EASTERN STATE. Governor Bodwell held a high and honorable position in the estimation of the people of this country. He was not a politician, in any sense of the word, but simply a plain business man, who had arisen to prominence by his industry, perseverance and strict attention to business. From small beginnings he had become one of the foremost business men of New England, engaged in vast enterprises in which he was a leader, not by any self assumed importance, but because men trusted him and his sagacious judgment. Though such was his standing in the business world, the quality of the man was best shown at his home in Hallowell, where he was looked up to as a friend of every one, and trusted by all as but few even are ever trusted.

ELLSWORTH AMERICAN. Hon. Joseph R. Bodwell of Hallowell, was a man well known to the people of this State as one who by indomitable perseverance, foresight and ability, created and maintained a varied business which not only brought wealth to himself, but gave remunerative wages to hundreds of his employes. In this way he became a real benefactor, for he helped men to help themselves, which is the best charity the world has ever known. He was a genuine alchemist, transmuting all he touched in a business way, even our granite hills, into gold.

FREE PRESS. By this dispensation the State loses a Chief Magistrate whose brief term in office had added to the great measure of respect and esteem which he had long enjoyed as a private citizen. His quick perception, clear judgment, strict sense of honor, firmness, and the courageous performance of every obligation, which had marked his career from youth to manhood and crowned his years with wealth and honor, promised to render Mr. Bodwell's administration as Governor one of the ablest and most successful in the State's history. It has been cut short by death; but not until it had forcibly illustrated how sterling, innate manhood may rise superior to adventitious circumstances of the most discouraging character.

Resolutions of Respect.

— — —

From a large number of resolutions passed by State organizations, city governments, and other civic bodies, the following are selected for publication:

MAINE STATE GRANGE.

WHEREAS, the Maine State Grange in common with all other associations, organizations and individuals in the State realize the irreparable loss we have all sustained by the removal from our midst of our honored and respected Chief Magistrate, Hon. Joseph R. Bodwell; and whereas, he was known to be in deep sympathy with the principles of our Order, and deeply interested in all our agricultural interests, it seems eminently fitting that we, members of the Maine State Grange, in annual meeting assembled, should place upon our records the sense of our great loss—therefore,

Resolved, That while bowing in obedience to the Supreme Will, we desire to affectionately express our appreciation of his worth, both as a man and as a ruler; of his eminent faithfulness to all trusts committed to his keeping, and of the great ability and honor with which he has discharged the arduous and responsible duties of his high office.

Resolved, That in the disinterested and generous spirit which marked his intercourse with all men; in the deep interest he has always taken in the working classes; in his great efforts towards the upbuilding of the State, and the good of all its citizens, he has written his name in kindness, love and mercy upon the hearts of thousands with whom he came in contact, and by whom his generous deeds and kindly acts will never be forgotten.

Resolved, That we extend our warmest sympathy to the family and immediate friends of our departed Chief Magistrate while yet the earth is fresh upon his coffin, and assure them that every heart throughout our whole State feels a large share in their personal sorrow.

Resolved, That these resolutions be inscribed upon our records and that a copy be sent to his family.

MAINE BOARD OF AGRICULTURE.

WHEREAS, The Board of Agriculture and citizens of Strong and vicinity, assembled in a Farmer's Institute, have received with feelings of profound sadness the telegram announcing the painful intelligence of the death of our chief executive, Governor Bodwell, therefore,

Resolved, That in his untimely and sudden death we realize that the State loses an able and conscientious Executive, an active business man, a faithful promoter of its agricultural interests, and a loyal friend of the laborer wherever found.

Resolved, That in this sad bereavement, we tender our deepest sympathy to the family and relatives of the deceased in their deep affliction, and to the many warm friends his wide business and social relations have won.

HALLOWELL CITY GOVERNMENT.

The City Council in joint convention passed the following resolutions:

WHEREAS, The Great Power Who rules us all has called from labor one of our most honored citizens, it is with profound sorrow and sadness we learn of the death of him whom the citizens of this State had learned to love as its Chief Magistrate; one whose large heart could take in matters of national importance, and still have room to consider the wants of the humblest poor; one whose name has stood for all that was honorable and manly among his fellows; a citizen of purest life and perfect integrity, whose name is destined to fill a conspicuous place in the history of our city, and of our State. Therefore,

Resolved, That our heartfelt sympathy be tendered to the bereaved family of our honored friend. They have lost one whose domestic virtues were no less distinguished than those of a public nature. May we hope that when the pain of their loss may be soothed by time, they may find comfort and consolation in the recollection that his memory is held in grateful affection by the hearts of his neighbors, his fellow citizens, and all who were brought into business connection with him.

Resolved, That in the death of Joseph R. Bodwell, this city has lost one of its greatest and truest friends, one who has been largely instrumental in adding to its prosperity, and who has always been ready to aid with his advice and counsel, his example and influence, all enterprises which would benefit the city both morally and financially.

Resolved, That we unite with citizens from all parts of the State in regarding his loss as a public calamity.

HALLOWELL CITIZENS.

At a mass meeting of the citizens, held Saturday evening, with Mayor Fuller as chairman, the following resolutions were unanimously adopted, which were drawn up by a committee, composed of Messrs. Beane, Rowell, Currier, Clary and Warner·

In citizens' meeting, assembled:

WHEREAS, By Divine Providence, one of our citizens has been called from our midst to live with those who have gone before in a brighter and happier home; and, whereas it is fitting and proper that the sympathy of neighbors and friends should be extended to the family and mourning relatives; Therefore,

Resolved, That in the death of our fellow citizen, Hon. Joseph R. Bodwell, we realize as only neighbors can, our great loss. Generous hearted and ever given to charity, many hearts now do and ever will revere his memory. Open and frank in his social relations, his death fills the hearts of all citizens with sadness. Manly and honest in his business affairs, his loss causes grief to his business associates. His pleasant smile and cordial greeting, in addition to his noble qualities, endeared him to all, and will ever keep his memory fresh in the minds of all who knew him.

Resolved, That to his mourning family we extend our heartfelt and sincere sympathy. With them we also mourn.

The secretary of this meeting, Mr. D. K. Jewell, was instructed to present a copy of the above resolutions to the afflicted family.

Mr. Beane offered the following resolutions:

In citizens' meeting:

Resolved, That it is the sense of this meeting that all business within the city should be suspended and all places of business remain closed Tuesday, December 20, the burial day of our honored citizen, Joseph R. Bodwell.

Unanimously adopted.

PORTLAND CITY GOVERNMENT.

Having assembled in joint convention, the Mayor presiding, Alderman Marks offered the following resolutions:

The Mayor, Aldermen and Common Council of the city of Portland, assembled in City Council upon the announcement of the death of the Governor of the State, appreciating the profound respect entertained for him personally by the citizens of Portland and sharing deeply in the general sense of public loss at the sudden close of his useful and honored life. Therefore.

Resolved, That the news of the death of the Chief Magistrate of our State, Honorable Joseph R. Bodwell, at his home in Hallowell this morning, is received by the city of Portland with the deepest regret; that his private life and personal character, his long and eminently successful and honorable business career and great influence in developing the resources and industries of Maine, his courage, energy and good judgment in protecting and managing large business enterprises, his broad and generous spirit and ready encouragement and aid to all that tended to serve the public interests, justly entitle him to respect and remembrance as a distinguished citizen who has deserved well of the State.

That he brought to the discharge of the duties of his high office all the resources of his practical experience and ability, a keen sense of the obligations and duties which the chief magistracy devolved upon him, a spirit of vigilant fidelity to every trust and an incorruptible honesty of purpose;—and that he leaves to his family and the State both in his private and his official life the legacy of an unsullied name.

That these resolutions be extended upon the records of the city and a copy of them be transmitted to Governor Bodwell's family as an expression of sincere and respectful sympathy.

BANGOR CITY GOVERNMENT.

At a largely attended meeting of the City Council Friday evening, called by Mayor Bragg to take appropriate action on the death of Governor Bodwell, the following resolutions were unanimously adopted:

Resolved, That the City Council of Bangor, in common with all citizens of Maine, has received with sincere sorrow, intelligence of the death of the Chief Magistrate of the State, and they desire on their own behalf and on that of the citizens of Bangor to express profound regard for the memory of the late Governor Joseph R. Bodwell, their appreciation of his high personal character, his exceptional capacity for office and his hearty and constant promotion of the moral and material welfare of his State. In his removal the State has lost a faithful and fearless officer, the industrial interests of the people an enterprising and inspiring leader, and the cause of moral reform an earnest an unswerving defender. His life illustrates the success under our free institutions possible to diligence and virtue, and presents to the rising generation an example full of encouragement and worthy of emulation. Such a life of prosperity honorably gained recalls the ancient proverb, "Man's character is his destiny."

Resolved, That the City Council tenders its hearty sympathy to the family of Governor Bodwell in this severe bereavement, which no human words can alleviate, but which will be illuminated by the ever present memory of the affectionate, generous life, whose termination they mourn.

GARDINER CITY GOVERNMENT.

It is fitting that the citizens of Gardiner should tender some tribute of their respect to the memory of their late Governor, whose remains are now lying in state at the Capitol.

I would therefore request that all places of business and all manufactories be closed between the hours of 11 A. M. and 2 P. M. of Tuesday, the 20th instant, at which time the last ceremonies in his honor will be performed.

A committee on behalf of the City Council and one representative of the citizens at large, will attend the funeral services at Augusta.

JOHN J. BERRY, Mayor.

A committee consisting of Hon. Joshua Gray, Hon. Wm. F. Richards, O. B. Clason, Esq., Henry Farrington, Esq., Capt. E. W. Atwood, G. W. Hezelton, Esq., were chosen to represent the citizens at large to attend the funeral services of Gov. Bodwell, and to act in connection with the committee from the City Council.

ROCKLAND KNIGHTS OF LABOR.

The following resolutions were passed by the Rockbound Assembly, Knights of Labor, at Vinalhaven, and are most significant and interesting as the members of that organization, almost without exception, are employes of the Bodwell Granite Company.

Resolved, That we profoundly mourn the sudden and untimely death of Hon. Joseph R. Bodwell, late Governor of the State of Maine, who for a third of a century has been so prominently identified with the business and progressive enterprise of the State of Maine and especially this town.

Resolved, That in his death we deplore the loss of an honest employer, whose simplicity of character endeared him to the poorest, one who was ever ready to listen to and redress the grievances of his employes, as was evidenced by agreements entered into between himself and this assembly.

Resolved, That his official acts, the signing of all the bills passed in the interests of the laboring people of the State while in the Governor's chair, have enshrined his memory in the heart of every true reformer in the State.

Resolved, That as a fitting testimony to the memory of our late employer, and to show in our humble way some appreciation of the services he has rendered to the cause of labor, we send one of our number to represent this assembly at the funeral and that a floral tribute be offered as a fitting tribute of our sorrow.

JOHN B. HUBBARD POST, G. A. R.

At the meeting of John B. Hubbard Post, No. 20, G. A. R., of Hallowell, held on Monday evening last, a committee was appointed to draft resolutions in honor of the memory of our departed Governor and fellow citizen. The following resolutions were submitted and unanimously adopted:

WHEREAS, By the dispensation of Divine Providence our honored Chief Magistrate and beloved citizen, Hon. Joseph R. Bodwell, has been taken from earth to his reward above, at a time when his services and influence seemed almost indispensable in carrying forward the public and business interests of this community and of the State, therefore,

Resolved, That we, as comrades of the Grand Army of the Republic, sincerely mourn the loss of one who was ever ready to extend to us a helping hand in carrying forward our benevolent enterprises, and in maintaining the principles so dear to every American citizen.

Resolved, That we sympathize deeply with his family in their sad bereavement, and assure them that the memory of the loved and honored husband, father and friend will ever be reverently cherished by an afflicted and sorrowing commonwealth.

Resolved, That a copy of these resolutions be furnished to the family of the deceased, and that they also be spread upon our records and published in the Hallowell Register and Kennebec Journal.

AUGUSTA CITY COUNCIL.

WHEREAS, Divine authority, in His mysterious wisdom, has deemed it well to call from his earthly labors our lamented Governor, Hon. Joseph R. Bodwell, it is considered proper that some expression of our sense of the great loss we have suffered thereby, should be made by this body. Therefore,

Resolved, That it is with the greatest sorrow that we have received the news of the death of the beloved Governor of our State; that in his life we recognize those sterling qualities of manhood which have made him a kind and loving husband and father; an honest and conscientious citizen; a pure, wise and incorruptible official, and a benefactor of his race. We deeply mourn his loss and extend our sympathy to his family in their great bereavement, and our commiseration to the people of the great State he loved so well and whose interests he did so much to promote and develop.

SONS AND DAUGHTERS OF MAINE IN LOWELL, MASS.

WHEREAS, The Great Governor of the universe has seen best to permit the departure from this world of the Hon. Joseph R. Bodwell, Governor of our native State of Maine, in the midst of his official responsibilities and in the ripened vigor of his mature manhood, whereby a great State is deprived of a noble citizen and a wise ruler, therefore,

Resolved. That we, the Sons and Daughters of Maine Association, in this city, place upon record our sympathy with our brothers and sisters in the loss they have sustained, and unite with them in our testimonial of the worth of so upright and honorable a man and ruler.

As one, in a special manner suited to represent the self reliant, honest, industrious, independent, ambitious and working character of the people of our native State.

As one, in himself, a noble example of what a young man can do, be, and become by correct habits, uprightness of character and patient toil, though commencing the journey of life in its humblest paths.

As one, who in himself, as a man was an example to laboring men by his own habits of toil, and also to business men by his honesty, fairness, promptness, faithfulness and public spiritedness, that work and upright-ness are the true secrets of success.

As one, who as a citizen, by his unaffected sympathy, his free and wise benevolence to the poor and all good objects, illustrated the nobility of unselfishness.

As one, who as a man cast the weight of his character, wealth and influ-ence in favor of whatever promoted the temperance, purity, good morals, education and building up of society.

As one, who as a ruler, though firm and independent in his convictions, was impartial and upright in his administrations, commanding the confi-dence and respect not only of his own party but of all the people.

In fine, *as one,* who in the varied relations of life, as a man, a citizen and a ruler, was an encouragement to the poor, an example to the rich, a friend to the needy, an aid to reform and an honor to the State; and whose death is a loss to humanity.

Resolved, That our sympathies are extended to our native State in the departure of so valuable a citizen; and to the family in the death of so true and affectionate a member.

Resolved, That these resolutions be spread upon our record book, a copy forwarded to the family of the departed Governor, the Senate and House of Representatives of Maine.

MILFORD LAND AND LUMBER COMPANY.

Resolved, That we, the stockholders of the Milford Land and Lumber Company, in annual meeting assembled, desire to give expression to our deep sorrow at the death of its leading spirit and constant friend as well as its honored President, Joseph R. Bodwell.

Resolved, That in all the relations he sustained with us, both personally and officially, he was always actuated by principles of the highest integrity and unswerving fidelity to all interests committed to his charge.

Resolved, That we will ever cherish his memory for his sterling qualities as a man; for his broad views and large abilities as a manager of affairs; for the great and active interest he always manifested for the prosperity of the community; and for his incorruptible character as Chief Magistrate of the State which loved and honored him for all these qualities combined.

BODWELL WATER POWER COMPANY.

Resolved, That the Directors of the Bodwell Water Power Company with unaffected sorrow profoundly mourn the death of its President, Joseph R. Bodwell.

Resolved, That in his death we sincerely deplore the great loss of the projector and efficient supporter of this company; that we desire on our own behalf, and that of all its members, to express our high regard and appreciation for his pure personal character, his extraordinary capacity for affairs, and his hearty and untiring efforts for the welfare of this association.

Resolved, That we sincerely concur in the truthful expressions of sorrow and mourning throughout the State, by its citizens, over its loss of an honest, resolute, and conscientious chief magistrate.

Resolved, That in his most useful and honorable career as the leader in the industrial interests of the State, and for the promotion of which his memory will ever be affectionately and gratefully perpetuated, he cannot be replaced.

Resolved, That to none of his works can we point more confidently than to this company, for evidence that he who has now gone from among us, full of years and honor, was a good and great man; genial in his nature, wise in judgment, truthful to the last degree, filled with noble impulses and doing with might whatsoever his hand found to do.

Resolved, That these resolutions be extended upon our records, and a copy furnished to his family, to whom we extend our heartfelt sympathy and condolence; and also that a copy be furnished to the press for publication.

BATH LODGE OF GOOD TEMPLARS.

WHEREAS, It has pleased our Heavenly Father in His mysterious providence to remove by death our beloved and highly esteemed Governor, Hon. Joseph R. Bodwell, and it becomes us in some suitable manner to recognize the event, therefore,

Resolved, That in the death of Governor Bodwell the temperance cause in this State has lost one of its firmest and most devoted advocates; one who was willing to make the largest sacrifices for the good of his fellow-men.

Resolved, That in his death we are called upon to put forth greater efforts in the cause, and by constant vigilance, unwearied perseverance, and examples of purity, emulate his virtues, and that we hear in this providence of God, a summons to a purer devotion to temperance than we have heretofore cherished.

Resolved, That we hereby tender our heartfelt sympathy to the family of our lamented Governor, and that this brief memorial be entered upon our records, and a copy of the foregoing preamble and resolutions be sent to the family of the deceased.

6

CITY OF LEWISTON.

WHEREAS, It has pleased our Heavenly Father to remove from our midst our Chief Magistrate, Joseph R. Bodwell;

WHEREAS, The citizens of Lewiston on hearing the sad announcement of his death unanimously expressed themselves, that the State had suffered a great loss. and the friends of temperance its noblest advocate;

Resolved, That the flags of the city be placed at half mast until after the obsequies of our deceased Governor.

Resolved, That these resolutions be spread upon the records of the City Council. and that they be published in the press of the city and a copy of them be forwarded to the family of our lamented Chief Executive.

Resolved, That out of respect to his memory we do now adjourn without the transaction of any further business.

THE NEW YORK AND BOSTON RAPID TRANSIT COMPANY.

WHEREAS, We are summoned to surrender our companionship with Governor Joseph R. Bodwell, late President of this Company, whose efficiency in the work of developing the great enterprise to which it is devoted cannot be expressed in any formal statement. and whose business example furnished a constant inspiration to us his associates and friends, therefore,

Resolved, That we unite in lamenting the decease of one who never failed to command our high respect and appealed to our deep affection by the inestimable qualities of his large and sympathetic heart.

That we testify together to our appreciation of the pure purpose and stainless integrity that stamped him as a man almost singular in the multitude with which he mingled, and,

That we sincerely join with the family and immediate friends of the deceased in deploring his unexpected departure, and tender them our deep sympathies in their heavy affliction, which must nevertheless be lightened with so many consolations.

Resolved, That this expression of our common sorrow be entered on the records of this Company and a copy of the same be forwarded to his bereaved family.

CITY OF BATH.

WHEREAS, We, the City Council of Bath, in convention assembled, learn with profound sadness of the death of Hon. Joseph R. Bodwell, Governor of the State of Maine. which occurred at his home in Hallowell on the 15th instant, and join with our sister municipalities in deploring the great loss sustained by our State, therefore,

Resolved, That in the death of Governor Bodwell, the State has lost an able, honest, earnest, upright, conscientious, faithful, unselfish and unassuming Executive; one who will be remembered as the honest politician, the sincere patriot, the faithful friend, the enemy of no one living.

Resolved, That the various industries of our State have lost one of their firmest and truest friends, for in Joseph R. Bodwell was combined experience, sagacity, public spirit, enterprise and strict integrity. so that he could command large resources to aid in any enterprise he might engage in.

He leaves to his family and the State of his adoption a life worthy of emulation by the young men of the country.

Resolved, That a copy of the resolutions be published in the daily papers and a copy be forwarded to the family of the deceased Governor, and that the flags of our city be kept at half mast until after the day of the funeral.

Resolved, That a committee of the City Government be appointed to attend the funeral of the deceased Governor.

Resolved. That the places of business in the city be requested to close during the hours of the funeral.

Messages of Condolence.

Many letters and telegrams of sympathy and condolence were received by the family, on the occasion of the death of Governor Bodwell, from various parts of the country, only a few of which can be inserted here. They were largely from business men in the principal cities, in New Orleans, New York, Philadelphia and Boston, with whom Mr. Bodwell had had large business transactions, and some were from State officials and business associates in Maine. The whole, of which the following are only samples, make up a tribute of respect which the death of few men in Maine or the country would have brought out.

ROCKLAND,
December 16th, 1887.

MRS. J. R. BODWELL.

Respected Madam:

I offer you most sincerely my heartfelt sympathy in this hour of your great trial and sorrow. I am fully aware that no words of mine can be of any consolation to you in this day of your great affliction.

Through the instrumentality of an all-wise Providence you are called to mourn the death of a dear and loving husband, and the State an honest, upright, intelligent, manly man. By the death of Governor Bodwell the State and the country has lost one of its foremost men, and we who knew him intimately in all the relations of life, a true and noble friend.

In this season of your bereavement it must be, and probably is, a consolation to you and your children that the people in every home of our State join in their condolence to you and yours in this great affliction. May God in His infinite mercy, give you strength and fortitude to bear the trouble that has so suddenly and unexpectedly visited your happy home. Again extending my sympathy to you and to your bereaved family,

I am, with great respect,

JOHN S. CASE.

BATES COLLEGE,
LEWISTON, MAINE, December 17, 1887. }

Dear Madam:

Allow me to tender you my sympathies in this hour of your great affliction. "Whom the Lord loveth He chasteneth."

No one can mourn as you; and yet I am safe in saying that the hearts of all the friends of temperance and good order in our beloved State are grief stricken by the death of Governor Bodwell, and they would gladly say this to you were it in their power.

Very truly,

MRS. GOVERNOR BODWELL.   O. B. CHENEY.

KEENE, N. H.,
December 19th, 1887. }

DEAR MRS. BODWELL:

Permit me to express, in these few lines, my deepest sympathy and feeling for you in the trying ordeal through which you are called to pass. I grieve that I am unable to stand among the large circle of friends who mourn the death of Governor Bodwell, and look upon the face of him who had so large a place in my heart. But circumstances beyond my control deprive me of that privilege. When I learned of your husband's illness, I daily visited his office in N. Y.; and being assured by hopeful reports, I took courage in the belief that, with his strong constitution, he would surely recover his health. So when the sad news of his death came, it gave me a shock from which I have not recovered.

Governor Bodwell was the most unselfish of men, and he was the embodiment of honesty. His kindness of heart was proverbial. In him I always found a warm and true friend ever ready to lend a helping hand, and I feel that I have met with a loss that cannot be made up. But my grief is nothing compared to the irreparable loss to his family, the community and the State. With greatest sympathy and regard,

I am sincerely yours,

S. W. HALE.

NEW YORK, December 17, 1887.

MY DEAR MRS. BODWELL:

I know that the words of a stranger cannot be of much value in the great affliction through which you are now passing. But on my own account I wish to place in your hands a slight record of the warm esteem I had for your late husband, and of my genuine sorrow for his loss.

He was a stranger to me until about one year ago, when I first met him in this city. Since that time our acquaintance has not been intimate. But I have seen enough of Joseph R. Bodwell to enable me to say that I have never met a more noble, generous or true hearted man. He seemed to me entirely incapable of any narrow or selfish act, and I know that his mind was incapable of entertaining a thought inconsistent with the very highest integrity. A late officer in the army, who had heavy contracts with him during the war, told me that he was the most *honorable* man he had ever encountered.

The country has few such men. Their death is a public as well as a private loss. I have no friend whose loss I could feel more deeply.

You, the companion of his life, who knew every secret of his heart, in the depths of your sorrow have at least the consolation of knowing that he lived a useful life, that he had gained the respect and affection of all who knew him and that he probably has not left behind him one single enemy.

Cordially yours,

L. E. CHITTENDEN.

MRS. BODWELL, Hallowell, Me.

HOUSE OF REPRESENTATIVES, }
WASHINGTON, D. C., December 16, 1887. }

MRS. J. R. BODWELL, Hallowell, Me.

Dear Madam:

Permit me to express to you my profound sympathy with you in the great grief which has overtaken you in the death of your husband.

The death of Mr. Bodwell, so great a loss to yourself, will be severely felt by his thousands of friends, who will mourn his departure from this life as a misfortune to themselves, our State and the country.

With sincere respect, very truly yours,

SETH L. MILLIKEN.

HOUSE OF REPRESENTATIVES, }
WASHINGTON, D. C., December 17, 1887. }

MRS. JOSEPH R. BODWELL.

Dear Madam:

I beg to offer you the heartfelt condolence of Mrs. Boutelle and myself, and to assure you of our sincere sympathy in the great affliction that has befallen you.

The death of your honored husband came to us as a severe shock, as we were led to hope by the reports that he was in a fair way to recovery.

I am painfully aware that no words can give any balm for such a sorrow as yours, but if anything could mitigate the pangs of such a swift bereavement, it would be the knowledge of the respect and esteem in which the departed was held by all who knew him, as Governor, citizen and friend. The State shares in your grief, and the loss of a strong and good man will be felt far beyond its limits.

Very respectfully yours,

C. A. BOUTELLE.

186 West Chippewa St., }
BUFFALO, Dec. 18, 1887. }

MRS. BODWELL:

Mrs. Dee and myself learned with feelings of profound sorrow and regret of the death of Gov. Bodwell. Since I made his acquaintance, in the year '76, I have always admired him for his many noble and manly qualities.

My personal relations with him were always pleasant and agreeable.

In your hour of affliction I send you this my humble tribute, with a prayer that the Great Comforter will aid you in bearing your great sorrow.

Mrs. Dee joins with me in sincere sympathy with yourself and family, for the loss of a kind-hearted husband and father.

Very respectfully yours,

JOHN F. DEE.

MY DEAR MRS. BODWELL:

It was with pain and grief that I learned of the death of your husband and my friend.

It was so entirely unexpected by me that the shock was great; what must it be to you!

Although my acquaintance with your husband was of comparatively recent date, yet such was his genial nature, that he immediately endeared himself to all that knew him, and I look back upon the friendship of our good Governor as one of the pleasantest of my life.

Though knowing well that no words can bring comfort to your stricken heart, yet I must express my deep sympathy for you and your family in this great affliction; ah, if words and sympathetic hearts could console you, then you might indeed be comforted, for from thousands of hearts and homes the truest and purest of sympathy is poured forth for you and the deepest regrets for the untimely death of so good and noble a man. He has left behind him an unsullied record, which is a precious legacy.

He has left a vacancy which can not easily be filled—it is a loss to our State—what must it be in his home!

I pray God may temper your affliction and give you strength to endure this great trial.

Assuring you of our deepest sympathy, I am

Most sincerely yours,

WILLIAM ENGEL.

BANGOR, December 17, 1887.

AUGUSTA, MAINE,
December 15, 1887.

MRS. JOSEPH R. BODWELL.

My dear Madam:

I have learned with great sorrow of the unexpected death of our Chief Magistrate, your most estimable husband, his Excellency Governor Bodwell.

As one who has long entertained towards him sentiments of highest esteem and respect, I venture to take the liberty of expressing to you and all the members of his bereaved family my most earnest sympathy.

I am, with great respect,
Very sincerely yours,

CHARLES W. DOHERTY.

218 Orange St.,
NEW HAVEN, Conn.,
Dec. 28, 1887.

MY DEAR MRS. BODWELL:

It is only our nearest and dearest to whom the privilege is given of bringing us what comfort they may in the first days of a great sorrow; and so I have waited a little before venturing upon any expression of my deep sympathy for you and yours. Even now I hesitate, because I am so much a stranger. In my visits, last summer, to my mother, Mrs. Hubbard, I have met you a few times, only. But if I seem an intruder, let me hope that the deep respect with which your husband inspired me, whenever I had a word with him, may plead my excuse.

This is no common loss which has befallen the public, for Gov. Bodwell was no common man. I met him first some years ago, when with my sister he canvassed the question of a building for the Hallowell Library. I remember what I afterwards said of him to her. I have never forgotten the cordial, honest, whole-souled man he seemed to me in that first interview, and the chance meetings I have since enjoyed have served to strengthen my confidence in his worth.

It is a noble and useful life that has thus suddenly ended here, but it is not for the good man himself that I grieve. Perhaps it is as he would have wished. Perhaps, as my own dear father, he would have chosen to go with powers untouched by age. My sorrow is not for him. It is for the State that has lost the guidance of that steady hand; for my native town, that must sorely miss her true-hearted citizen; most of all, for the home he loved and gladdened. I know how much must have gone from you with him. Accept the sympathy I can poorly frame in words.

Very sincerely,

VIRGINIA H. CURTIS.

DEAR MRS. BODWELL:

I have just read of your sad bereavement and my heart aches for you and Mrs. Paine, and my own sorrow is brought freshly to my mind. I wish that it were in my power to say something that might be in some measure a help to you now; but the mission of sorrow cannot be understood by us poor mortals while our grief is fresh, and time, only, performs for us the chastening work that our good Father intends. Human sympathy was very grateful to me in my trouble, and that you have mine now be assured. With love for yourself and Mrs. Paine,

Your sincere friend,

A. L. METCALF.

141 East 16th St., New York, Dec. 17th, 1887.

VASSALBORO', Dec. 19, 1887.

DEAR MRS. BODWELL:

It is vain for me to attempt to offer consolation in this, your terrible affliction; but I wish to express something of the sorrow we feel at the death of Gov. Bodwell. During the past years he, by his kindness, has endeared himself to each member of our family. How well I remember when, four years ago, at Indianapolis, my own father's life hung as by a thread. Mr. Bodwell stood by and helped me to care for him till mother could come. Six months later, when our dear Will was so suddenly taken, Mr. Bodwell came to us quickly as possible, and we felt that his great heart was moved in sympathy for us. And now we each feel a personal loss and grief. Father and Clara were fully intending to go to Hallowell yesterday, but because of father's feeble condition and the severity of the storm, they very reluctantly gave it up.

Please give kindest regards to Mrs. Paine, and say how our hearts ache for her in her great sorrow.

With feelings of deepest sympathy, in which all here join,

I am yours truly,

ANNIE O. BURLEIGH.

ROCKLAND, Dec. 15th, 1887.

MRS. J. R. BODWELL.

My dear Madam:

Please accept my sincere sympathy for you in your heavy affliction. We all feel deeply for, and join with you in mourning the irreparable loss which you have sustained. Expressions of sorrow and sympathy for you are universal. Nothing more can be said on so sad an occasion as this than to express the hope that the knowledge that every citizen of the State deplores and keenly feels your sudden bereavement, may tend in some slight degree to lighten your burdens and alleviate your sorrow.

I remain very sincerely yours,

C. E. LITTLEFIELD.

NORWAY, ME., Dec. 15th, 1887.

MY DEAR MRS. BODWELL:

My heartfelt sympathy goes out in your behalf at the great loss you have sustained by the death of your kind husband. I condole with you most sincerely on the sad event, and be assured that all who knew him share in your sorrow at this hour.

A kind husband and father, a good counsellor and friend, has passed on to enjoy the reward of a well-spent life.

Commending you to Him who doeth all things well, I remain

Yours sincerely,

GEORGE L. BEAL.

A telegram was received from Governor Sawyer of New Hampshire, and Governor Ames of Massachusetts sent the following note to Governor Marble:

COMMONWEALTH OF MASSACHUSETTS,
EXECUTIVE DEPARTMENT,
BOSTON, Dec. 20, 1887.

MY DEAR SIR:

I deeply regret that my official duties are such that I cannot attend the obsequies of your predecessor in office, the Hon. Joseph R. Bodwell. I shall be represented thereat by my Adjutant General, Samuel Dalton, and by other members of my military staff. Personally I am grieved at the death of so able, energetic, earnest and honest a man as Governor Bodwell, and officially I can say that the people of this commonwealth have heard with sorrow that one who was of their number and who had attained such eminence by force of worth, has at a comparatively early time been called away from the affairs of earth in which he dealt so wisely. Assuring you of my best wishes for your success and happiness in your official career, I am yours sincerely,

OLIVER AMES,

Governor of Massachusetts.

NOTE.—On page 8, it is stated that Hon. Moses Webster died at Rockland. It should have been at Vinalhaven, where he ever resided after he came to Maine.